THE
CLARION

THE CLARION

Nina Dunic

Invisible Publishing
Halifax & Toronto

Library and Archives Canada Cataloguing in Publication
Title: The clarion / Nina Dunic.
Names: Dunic, Nina, author.
Identifiers: Canadiana (print) 20230168671
                   Canadiana (ebook) 20230168809
                   ISBN 9781778430282 (softcover)
                   ISBN 9781778430299 (HTML)

Classification: LCC PS8607.U537 C53 2023 | DDC C813/.6—dc23

Edited by Diane Schoemperlen
Cover and interior design by Megan Fildes | Typeset in Laurentian
With thanks to type designer Rod McDonald

Invisible Publishing is committed to protecting our natural environment. As part of our efforts, both the cover and interior of this book are printed on acid-free 100% post-consumer recycled fibres.

Printed and bound in Canada.

Invisible Publishing | Halifax & Toronto
www.invisiblepublishing.com

Published with the generous assistance of the Canada Council for the Arts, the Ontario Arts Council, and the Government of Canada.

everything
always
for douglas

MONDAY

I ADJUSTED my tie upward, firming the knot, tightening its snug grip on itself. Satisfying. But the knot was too high; I loosened and pulled it gently down again, and it relaxed, expanded. I enjoyed the adjustments; ties were among the last male adornments left. These long silk trimmings bound around our necks, just for a stripe of colour on our chests. Everything else being ordinary and every other day being the same, the adornment meant I was not those things today—ordinary or the same. I wore a tie to every audition and I took my time adjusting it, looking in the mirror, breathing.

More than twenty years ago I had come home from school and Grandma was sitting there in the kitchen, talking with my mother, her big hands on the table, veined and rough and strong. Her profile was absolute against the pale wall; she had a sharp nose, sharp jaw—face shapes from when life was quieter but harder. I knew her as a solid woman complicated by wincing, dark grey eyes, as if she was a little bit shy, a little unsure, even as she was calmly efficient in all things. The trumpet stood between them on the table. It was tarnished, a fragmented gold colour, an entirely incongruent and absurdly upright object in the pale green kitchen. It took me out of the moment, coming home from school, the sharp smell of coffee in the room, the cool mint colour of the walls.

I liked to remember that scene with my grandmother because it was grounding. My audition was at three o'clock. I always woke up a little strange on the morning of an audition—I'd done it often enough that the more violent shakes of performance anxiety had left my body, but I still felt heightened. Faint electricity, silvery and light, running through my limbs, little sparks fading in the corners of my mind. And I still remembered the scene from more than two decades ago: the schoolbag on my back dropping behind me, soundless. Too shy to have attention turn to me, I did not like to interrupt adults. Later I learned the trumpet should never stand like that, but should rest in its case. Grandpa had fought in the war and bought the trumpet when he got back, teaching himself to play. He was dead now and it would go to me, my grandmother said. My sister Stasi did not want it.

I remember I was stunned by the twisting gold metal in our kitchen—machine-like but elegant, a muscular beauty—and what followed was years of learning, playing, performing and trying. Trying very hard, often. But it was not in my nature to try hard for things, to arch myself, to reach for something; I felt sometimes I was misshapen by all this, the auditions and the trying. Maybe as a child I felt a bit of dread. Or maybe, years later, I've coloured the memory with how I feel now.

I caught the bus and sat close to the back, my case resting across my lap. The bus was almost empty. I didn't want to walk to the subway; the sidewalks were patchy with small islands of ice, and I had slipped the day before. I didn't fall to the ground, just that sharp wobble that got my blood up.

I sat facing a young woman on the bus; she had one glove off and she was inspecting her nails. She looked at them closely, then from a distance, removing her second glove, taking a minute with her other hand. Her nails did not seem to be painted and I could not tell what she was looking for. Her eyes flicked over to me, sharp and narrowing, and I turned away embarrassed—I was not welcome, even as an observer, in her world. A cold flash ran through me. I realized she was pretty, but she was mistaken, I did not stare at pretty people: too often their faces had turned hard and bored. Outside the bus I saw a group of teenagers on the sidewalk, laughing, followed by another group of teenagers, plodding. It was just after two o'clock. They were out on the streets, liberated and drifting.

I had rehearsed the songs, mostly in the mornings. At night I sometimes played them again, a little looser. But I had also rehearsed my thoughts—lined them up, walked through them—a way of aligning how I felt. You should know the purpose. Yours and everyone else's. When you stand up to play a piece, you should know why you're there, why the audience is there, what it feels like to play it, what it feels like to hear it, and everything that came before—who wrote it, when, and why. That was the way I approached it and always had. But I knew others who did not approach it this way and, disoriented, I saw that they were still very good, even better than me. But it was the only way I knew how to do it.

My purpose today was to get the job—get paid, stay the winter—be energized, vigorous, interesting for them. Their regular trumpeter had gone to Europe for the season; I didn't know anything about him, we had never crossed paths. The job was two nights a week in the west end at an expensive restaurant with modern Mediterranean cuisine—but younger, edgier than most restaurants in the area—and the live band was prominent on the website. It was a draw. I wondered about the clientele. The pay was good and I knew they would be auditioning several players—probably Ollie, if he was still free on Friday and Saturday nights, probably Erick. Ollie was impressive physically, tall and bulky in the shoulders, with a strong and interesting profile. On trumpet, he was brash, elbowing others aside; some people liked that. He would be the one in my way.

The bus stopped and picked up a stooped old woman. She wore a nest of scarves tied around her head and neck; briefly I imagined her tying them carefully before she left the house, like me. But her small face peered out, uncomfortable on the bus, impatient for her journey to be over—a sad and tired figure. I looked away from the woman. I knew that seeing her would change how I felt, and I needed to feel a certain way for this.

The clientele at the restaurant would be trendy, I guessed—dressed up for the night. The women would have large bracelets and red lips, and the men would be trim in dark colours. Their purpose would be to have an authentic experience. They were dining out and would take pictures and video, but the music would be a moment they couldn't capture as well on the phone—the sound was never right—

so they would feel it was something elusive and important. I wasn't sure what they would know or care about the music itself. The short set list I'd been sent included a holiday song; OK, it was November, it made sense, but I hoped they didn't get too heavy with them. Once holiday songs hit the grocery stores, I don't think anybody wants to hear the cover that night over dinner, unless it's pulled way back, way down. Circling around it, almost unrecognizable. Otis Redding's "White Christmas"—that way.

I was auditioning alone, no band, they said; I would be auditioning for the restaurant owner. Performing for someone like that, I knew the trumpet itself would not be the focus, it would be me. How I looked and carried myself, how I felt about myself. And that was the tricky thing, wasn't it—I felt good about myself when I wasn't thinking about it, but now I would be thinking about it, and that would turn it all inside out. The others who were good at it, the practised uncaring—the suspicion they were not comfortable either but good at lying, better at lying—I was pushing against that slowly seeping resentment of those who were better at lying.

Those were not helpful thoughts, and I knew that already; I knew almost everything about this but still I would cycle through the same things—knowing something does not make it stop. The bus was pulling into the subway station. There was a subtle twitching under my skin, light currents of adrenaline starting to circulate; performance, self-consciousness, trying to remain inside my body, inside the moment, while my mind was pulling me out. I saw myself from the outside, saw how others might see me. Old turns. I breathed, a full push from my lungs.

The old woman was still standing near the front of the bus and I got up and stood behind her. My legs felt loose but still good. Sometimes it was the legs that bothered me more than anything. I focused on the pattern of her scarves—she had many, unmatching: green with a yellow pattern, dark blue and black, red and purple, red and yellow, mostly stripes, sometimes curving lines or florals. The case was a pleasing weight in my hand as I stepped off the bus and walked through the station—my expensive shoes clipping against the concrete, a hard sound with purpose—and jogged lightly down the steps into the subway, my legs loose and good.

I stood on the platform, conscious of my posture and keeping straight-chested. The subway track was a dark tunnel disappearing around the corner. I wasn't in the mood to look at other people, but I did; it was better if I pressed myself to see them. It pulled me back into the moment. A couple stood ahead of me, not talking to each other: the man was looking at his phone, the woman's face was lifted toward the screen that showed headlines. He was wearing dress pants and shoes, with a long coat, black. He had a good profile, elegant. But he also had a goldfish mouth, a reverse scoop turning sharply down at the edges, making him seem vaguely dissatisfied—and dull. The woman wore tall boots, black, narrow-heeled; a striking silhouette against the platform's long stretch of beige tile. Her coat was navy blue, and her thin blond hair brushed the tops of her shoulders. She read the headlines impassively, lips pressed together. She may have been dull as well—a mid-level manager somewhere bland, somehow tied up with the goldfish guy. She glanced back at him briefly, but he did not look up from his phone. She started to rummage in her bag.

The tunnel rumbled as a train approached; I looked along the tunnel's curve and saw that the train was mine. It pulled in and slowed to a stop, sighing. I walked in, glancing around for seats, then sat by the window. We started to move through the dark tunnels. There were a few people around, but most had their backs to me. One woman sat so close that if I looked at her it would have been a confrontation; we kept our eyes several feet apart.

People-watching my whole life—at first, I thought it was a shy kid's way of understanding who to be, how to belong. Watching the other animals to run with them, something like that. When I was a kid, a neighbour's dog had a litter of puppies and I'd spent afternoons sitting with them in his yard; most of them ran, all chaos and energy, but some of them watched. Now it was deliberate for me. It's how I pulled my mind off its circular track; left alone, my mind would gnaw only on itself. An audition, anxieties on loop. My thoughts darted quickly, hurried along by the quick-moving blood in my arms and legs; I needed something else to think about.

I wondered about the restaurant owner. Who was he? A money man or an art man? I had to assume the latter, as there were better ways to make money than paying a live band two nights a week. A music lover, a man of taste—maybe from the old world. An immigrant or the son, thinking art was more than an adornment, it was life itself, a grasp at meaning beyond ordering boxes of meat and endless cycles of dishes. I could get along with an owner like that. And I had already recognized the drummer from the band photo—it was Boris. I had known him socially some time ago, five or six years back, when I used to go to bars with a few musicians and their friends, when I was trying out the community. I respected how he played.

I watched stations slide past.

I remembered Boris's face was sclerotic, ancient acne scars so catastrophic he may well have been disfigured as a young man, a good reason to hide behind a drum set, to smash things. But there was no anger in his movements—I remember he had great, loose arms, played calm and thoughtful, relaxed, standing somewhere behind the moment and not asserting himself, letting the rhythm slide through him instead. I respected that.

It was my stop. I stood up and waited at the doors before they pulled open. The station and platform were green and white, cleaner than where I had got on.

A young man was also getting off the train ahead of me; he had a bulky backpack and salt-stained shoes—a college student maybe. Or a courier. A nervous traveller who carried half his life with him. I heard my own shoes again, clean cracks of sound against the platform tile; I walked slowly, deliberate, solidifying my legs against the sparking nerves. Any time my thoughts were interrupted I felt a great pull, like suction—back toward that tingling fear. Auditioning, performing, people carefully looking at me and me carefully pretending they weren't. My delicate refusal of self-consciousness. The inner tumult to reach it.

I surfaced from the subway and stood on a street corner surrounded by a bank, a restaurant, another restaurant, and a bar. A lot of competition here, on the corner at least. Orienting myself, I knew I'd have to cross, turn right, and walk only four or five minutes.

There were some fears I would have to dispel quickly.

My first fear: I would walk in there and introduce myself and somehow stumble or confuse my words. That rarely happened and, when it did, people forgot quickly. It's the last impression that matters, more than an early stumble—just deliver a good shake and a genuine smile before you leave. That was the moment. And the smile is always easy then because I'm relieved at the end, washed away by the rush of release.

Another: I would mess up the performance. I snuffed this out quickly because I never have—not once. There were notes brashly played and phrases that did not end how I wanted, how was best, but not here. Remote imperfections were nothing to a restaurant owner, who was likely not a musician of any kind, let alone a trumpet player. The instrument itself was alien to them; my expensive shirt and shoes were already more important. My confidence. Minor slips could be eclipsed by confidence—a truth that turned my self-consciousness elsewhere.

The last fear: they would not care. It was rare, but I had to fight this fear the hardest. I'd only been to two auditions where they did not care—both managers, trying to organize a shoot and an event—but those auditions struck deep. I bored them when I walked in, I bored them when I played; they didn't stand up to shake my hand, their smile was a grimacing pullback of skin on their face. Remote and bloodless, a cold white moon for me to perish on. I could take almost anything but one of those again. Why did any of us do this—find our instruments, relearn how to breathe, learn to read the scribbling language on the page, play it again and again and again and again? And again. Why any of that? In a world of wars and disease and death. This was something that mattered in a way that also didn't matter; we were supposed to be together in it—in believing it might matter. The people who did not care were a humiliation, showing a cold truth.

Salottino. I had walked a few steps past the door before seeing the sign. The salt on the sidewalk crunched under my heel as I turned back for the entrance. The outside brick was painted black and the letters were red; the name was across the glass in cursive letters and, smaller, just above the door. Number 889 in gold numbers. Here we go.

I stepped inside. The door fell shut heavily behind me. The front of house was empty so I walked past the first rows of tables and closer to the bar. The restaurant was both long and deep, wide open save for a few columns covered on all sides with tall mirrors, an expansive room that would move sound well. I was impressed with the ceilings. They had been raised; I hadn't noticed from the outside, but they had clearly jacked up the height after the entrance—they must own the building. The colours were dark, almost entirely blacks and reds. All hues of red: bright, deep, or bruised with purple. It was disorienting, coming in from the bright afternoon, as if I had descended into another world, a deeper one.

And the stage—which my eyes had darted around, trying to see everything else first, evasive and shy of where I knew I'd be standing—glittered in blue. Plates of blue glass lined the wall behind the stage, with a matching painted floor, and cool lights bathed the raised circular platform in a sapphire glow.

A man came out of the backroom, wearing black slacks and a slim-cut black shirt. He was short and muscular, around fifty, with a round, well-lined face. His fading hair was closely cropped. "Peter?" he asked.

"Yes, that's right," I said.

"Al." He extended his hand to shake mine. "Alessandro. Good to meet you."

I looked around again. "The ceilings in here—great." I phrased it poorly, but Al nodded and looked up and around with me.

"Yes, cut it and built it up years ago. Decades now? I can't tell anymore." Al smiled. "What are decades? Nothing."

I felt good about Al. A money man or an art man? I couldn't tell yet, but the audition was already promising. I had lost track of something to say and a brief silence settled. I set down the trumpet case gently, a way of doing something in that moment.

"I'll get her," Al said, still smiling. "I'll let her know you're here. Just have a seat if you want." Al turned and left.

Her? So it wasn't Al. The chairs were stacked upside down on the table tops; I pulled one down and sat on it, arranging my case beside me, not because I wanted to sit but because he had made the suggestion. I looked around. I already knew but suddenly I felt it—there was no band here, I was auditioning alone. Present now in the room, I felt a flash of fear. Real fear, a caught breath and sudden drop. A cramp in my abdomen. Alone on that stage?

She came out almost immediately. She was younger than I was expecting for an owner—forties? Early forties. Late thirties, even. She also wore all black, but had a grey apron she was removing as she came from the back. Her face was severe, squarish with a broad forehead, a hard jaw. For a moment I thought she was mean, but her eyes were large and alive, and the lines around her mouth showed emotions ready on the surface; sensitivity and warmth were waiting there. She was complex. I stood to shake her hand.

"Hi," I said. "I'm Peter." I paused, then quickly added, "Trumpet."

"Yes, of course." She smiled. "My name is Lucia."

We shook hands. I nodded without saying anything. Her eyes were fixed on me and brightly curious, but also sharp; I felt shy. I was not even thinking about playing for her; simply facing her felt immense. My mind was suddenly noisy, wordless.

She turned, walked away, and pulled down a chair from a nearby table. She brought the chair over, flipped it gently, and sat on it, facing me. I sat back down. "Do you have any questions?" she asked. "We tried to put as much information as possible in the posting. But you know—if you have any questions." I could tell she was already sizing me up. "Let me know, I can answer."

"No, actually," I said. My mind sped through a few responses but nothing was right. I thought I should say something, but I couldn't. "No, I don't have any questions. I'm good."

She looked at me, taking a few moments to decide what to say. "Are you sure you don't have any questions?"

I was confused by her asking again; now I knew I had to ask something. "When did you raise the ceilings on the building?"

Her eyes widened briefly before she smiled. I could tell she hadn't been asked that before.

"I didn't, actually," she said. "My mother did it in the eighties. Half this block was owned by one family—came from Greece, big farms and orchards back home, money in the family—and my mother had a good relationship with them. She financed it, of course, but she had to convince them."

Lucia was looking around the room, like Al did when I had first come in.

"A long time ago now. Honestly, during the big storms, it leaks. The edges." She pointed around the room where the ceiling had been propped up. "I don't think they sealed it well enough, and something has broken down over time. It doesn't come into the room, just the edges look damp. I've been ignoring it for about a year, but there'll come a time when I can't ignore it anymore."

I nodded, looking around with her, but I couldn't think of anything to say. I didn't know about roofs or waterproofing; I wanted to offer something about the building—the way sound moves, what that meant to me—but my mind had gone white.

"Anyway," she said. "Go ahead and set up near the mic." She stood up from her chair and gestured toward the stage. "I'm sorry we couldn't get the whole band here. We have to play something on the system instead."

"Do you mind if I use the bathroom first?" I asked. "It was a long commute."

"Of course," she said, pointing to the back. "Just over there, down the hallway."

"I'll just leave the trumpet here," I said, removing my coat and hanging it on the back of the chair.

"Sure. I'll set up the first song."

I stood and walked around the edges of the room to the back. In the bathroom I felt calmer, alone in a small space, but still there were waves of adrenaline rippling through me. Alone on that stage—auditioning without a live band. It wasn't typical for nightclub gigs—usually they brought in the band for the day and went through a player each hour, got feedback from the others, felt how it all fit together. That was supposed to be part of it. And knowing Boris would have been a comfort. I went into a stall, and the cramp turned into a painful rush of my bowels—out, out. I winced but it was finished quickly, there wasn't much left anyway. A palm print of sweat was forming on my chest, but I was lighter.

I stood in front of the mirror, washing my hands. Suddenly my own face was foreign to me: an off-colour mask, the tie sad and cloying. Fear was trying to take over. I ran my hands under cold water—ice cold—which took my mind away from my legs, from the softly gathering weakness at the knees. The cold water grew painful, and I took a few deep gasps of air, then pushed them out hard. Keep the legs good and the chest open. Keep the shoulders loose. I turned the water hot and brought the blood back to my hands, letting the pain sear for half a second, then another second more. I shut the tap. Breathing full, hands throbbing, the rest of my body forgot the fear.

I came out of the bathroom and smiled at Lucia; she smiled back. I retrieved my trumpet and brought it to the stage; she was sitting, alone, six or seven tables back. She propped one arm on the table and crossed her legs in front of her, ankle on knee, with a gentle tilt to her head. It was a friendly posture, almost casual, but she assumed it carefully, watching. I opened the case, pulled out the trumpet, and turned from her and the mic, facing the back of the stage, holding it and running my fingers over the valves a few times, a loosening of my hand. The metal was cool. I had to remind myself of what I knew. I could play. The notes were pure, existing outside my body. I knew how to deliver them cleanly. I knew all of this already.

I turned back to face Lucia. "Okay," I said. "You can start the first one."

She gestured behind her to the dark corners of the restaurant.

"Crimson and Clover." I knew this one so well—where to wander, where to linger. I closed my eyes and stiffened my legs briefly, locking my knees, then releasing them again.

My legs felt strong, a solid base for my breath. She wanted the trumpet as the vocal, wanted me to feel it out. I had practised endlessly. The song's gentle stroll started up; I released the first note, bright, just a beat late. The song was nearing fifty years old, and in a dim room it would transform every face in half-shadow. People would look around in wonder. Cocktails would sparkle. It was shaggy, shy-eyed, and mournful—stumbling gently into rhythm. Tommy James, born Tommy Jackson, a boy of twelve forming his first band. Tommy, whose songs other artists took to fame.

I looked up into the empty space in the room, above where Lucia sat. I released the notes, corners tight, then pulled back my breath and released the next, like a slow wheel going round. I kept my knees soft and my shoulders loose. It felt OK. It was better at home. This morning at home, Tommy would have been proud—I wasn't obsessive, precision was dull, I shook out some shy longing. I knew this song so well because of my father, after the record player broke down, selling our records in boxes for a few bare dollars; then, years later, realizing he was wrong and buying a new record player. Going to shops to find his favourites again. Tommy James and the Shondells were from my father's youth, but this song was different from the others somehow, warming the living room sometimes in the afternoons, changing the colour of the light.

But auditions were disfiguring; I was tighter and stiffer in every direction. Then the anxious grasp at ignoring that. Playing to look loose when I was not. I focused on breaths—big and round, big and round, the song wandering away into its last note. Crimson and clover, over and over.

It was okay. I smiled at Lucia, the first time I had looked at her since I started. I tried to be bright but felt a rueful pull at the edges of my mouth. She had a straight face that softened when our eyes met.

"I've always loved that one," I said, approaching the mic and speaking into it; my voice boomed across the room. Awkward, I pulled back from the mic and spoke around it. "My father had that record."

"It's aged well, right?" she said. "It has a nice patina now. Nostalgic. And I like to hear the trumpet up front like that."

I nodded, smiling. I liked how she said "patina" and, in liking that, felt shy again. My eyes fell away and down to the floor in front of her, between the tables, a lightly polished black tile.

The next song was starting. The Stones, "I Got the Blues."

I had been working on it for a while, a vintage bluesy amble, nice and slow, nothing showing around the edges. An end-of-nighter, carried gently. The Stones, though: unfathomable worlds, from dark clubs to apocalyptic arenas, the women, the drugs—nothing a mortal could access. But they did, everyone did. In every car radio and dive bar in the country. Shiny-faced drunks and tie-loosened suits, both pounding the tables to a Stones song—the rest of us between them, thinking the Stones spoke for us too. It wasn't possible. Somewhere there was a lie; I could never find it.

And then this simple thing, "I Got the Blues."

I took my first notes as slowly as I could, tightness still shadowing me, and played them straight. Mick's voice went long, and I followed—backing trumpet, played live over the recording, transformed the song. The empty club, filled with small polished tables floating above a dimly gleaming floor, all black and red, started to blur. Something like a lonely memory, maybe someone else's—a flashing bite of gin, people going home alone, people going home with strangers, fake-happy, sad. And who was I? Playing the Stones. Virtually a virgin, a nobody, a man at the back, unremembered. Pretty much everybody, I was everybody. Not quite sad but going home as unimportant as a Tuesday afternoon.

The song ended. I had lost track and it ended. I lowered the trumpet and did not look at her to force the smile; I felt apart.

I saw a spot on the bell and lifted my tie to smooth it away—moisture, a droplet on the brass. I lifted my eyes to look at Lucia and saw her body unmoved, still sitting in that watchful, careful pose, still a soft tilt to her head. She was a terror to me—not specifically her, but a watcher, any watcher—and that drew something closed that otherwise would have been open. Years spent trying to keep it open—denied. I took a deep breath and another, then a fuller one. Then I smiled at her. The song was good, I had done enough.

She smiled back. "Ready for a Christmas one?"

"Always," I said. There was a wry *hah* in her face.

"White Christmas," Bing's version. I liked it a little sad—instead of the jaunty nod at regret—I liked something vague left unfinished in the air. Bing was always winking at you. Bing enjoyed everything. Maybe that wasn't fair: it was the forties, that's what they wanted, equanimous and clean-cut, something like a big-band host. Maybe that's why it seemed like all these guys were alcoholics. But I liked "White Christmas" vague and pulled back—I left notes short and tapering softly, with unhurried spaces between. Something immaculate a trumpet could do. It was a simple song, wistful, short, and then it was over.

I lowered the instrument and wiped my mouth quickly with my left hand, a habit when I was relieved. "It's a classic," I said. "I guess we're done."

"Thank you." Lucia stood up. "Thank you for coming in."

I saw her standing there, and the pale circle of her face, but I avoided looking directly at it. I didn't want to read her face. I could not bring myself to look, did not want to know, not standing right in front of her. Not as two live things, facing each other. I wanted to know later—a call, a message—while alone. I wanted to go home with the relief of the audition over and not knowing how it might end.

I wiped the mouthpiece quickly with a cloth and placed everything back in my case, flipping the top back and clicking it shut, crouching close to the floor. She was still standing; I could see her only in the corner of my vision. An upright figure among the tables.

I felt better. Better for a few moments and then, sharply, rocketing upward, better than drugs. A soaring lightness in my chest. Everything tight slackened so suddenly I felt I could slip off the stage without my body at all, a movement of sound itself—arms and legs nothing more than air.

Endorphins, adrenaline, dopamine, cortisol, norepinephrine—the cleanest drugs out there. If you want to get high, perform for a stranger, finish, breathe, and walk out. You will drown in absolution, in shimmering waterfalls of relief.

I clipped lightly down the steps of the stage, holding my case in my right hand. I gripped the handle more firmly than usual, feeling the tight pleasure of muscle. My chest and shoulders—beautiful. Everything tight and real as my body came into focus with relief; a good smile and shake was the end, and now it was so easy.

Lucia was still standing there. I felt present for the first time standing and facing her; I was taller, a foot at least. Her hair was parted down the middle, tied back, plain as someone who worked in a kitchen. I wanted to ask for her last name but I didn't. I could find it later. I started putting on my coat.

"Thank you for the opportunity to audition," I said, reaching out my hand.

"Peter, the pleasure is mine. Thank you. Thank you for coming," she said, shaking my hand. Her eyes fell briefly to my side. I wondered if she was shy, or disappointed. It didn't matter now, of course. I didn't want to know. "I appreciate you taking the time," she said, our hands falling apart.

"This is all I do," I said. "I work in a restaurant and I play trumpet." I was still smiling into her face, feeling suddenly intimate, suddenly able to talk. "It's all I know."

"Yes, of course, I understand," she said. "We will call everyone on Thursday."

I started walking out—past the dozens of tables, too small, crowded together—and I flew through the heavy front door. The cold air outside lit up my face and fired through my lungs.

I liked Lucia. There was something honest and plain about her—a heaviness, almost. I suspected she was significant. I didn't fully know what that meant; I only sensed its weight at a distance.

The sidewalk was crusted with ice softly breaking apart, and hard bites of salt. All of it felt good. I crunched loudly as I walked, both hearing and feeling the sound beneath my shoes.

I descended into the dusty throat of the subway, blurred figures streaming past in both directions. The train platform was crowded with restless outlines; I couldn't seem to focus. I liked Lucia and wanted her to like me back. I wanted to get the gig. I wanted the money and wanted her to think I was good and watch me, two nights a week, on the stage with the band. I knew I would be better then, standing behind the sax, Boris behind me. I knew how loose and large I would feel by not being alone. I knew about Tommy and Mick and Bing and how they sounded with a ceiling raised like that—how the red room in low light would make people fall in love with strangers two tables over. Not romantic love, the better kind. I knew how live music felt, not just sounded. How some eyes in the room would inexplicably start shining. Three songs with no backing band was hard for me to show her. Did she know that?

The subway was busier now as the train pulled in, crowded with figures just beginning to take shape as my blood started to steady and slow. Relief was still hot within me—I could sprint alongside the train in the tunnels, and imagined it briefly: my feet snapping hard in a dark tunnel, both arms going, the trumpet left somewhere behind, safe. It was ludicrous, like an action movie, but appealing. So often my body lay dormant, but when ignited with the right combination of stress and relief, I was boundless, weightless—I was aerated fire, consumed with incredible power.

I got on the train, rested my case on the floor between my feet, and held on to a pole above my head. I was starting to see people again. Red rain boots on an old woman—exquisite. A young girl with a bike helmet covered in butterflies, her small face beneath it, her mouth side-chewing on the chin strap that pressed into a plump cheek. Two teenagers in skinny jeans with expensive headphones slung around their necks, their impervious expressions, that adolescent assumption they should be apart from the rest of us. I loved how much they knew, how little they knew. And then all working-age adults, twenties and thirties and forties and older, everyone a little tired, a little bored, most faces tipped down into their phones. We would avoid interaction at all costs, but a rare interruption—*Pardon me, is this the right stop?*—and we'd break open, helpful and eager.

I looked into the dark glass I was facing and saw my reflection, a round face with high cheeks, soft chin, unimportant nose. Some musicians looked truly interesting but I looked like a quiet guy who worked in a kitchen. I couldn't grow a proper beard; my hairline was fading at the corners. Someone once said I looked like this one actor, a lesser-known guy but I knew his name and a movie or two—he was always cast as the round-faced guy who didn't matter.

I got off the train at my stop and decided to walk. My high was mellowing into a post-euphoric calm; the audition wasn't so bad. I might have been tight in my chest and on the notes, but I had pushed through it, and perhaps Lucia never saw. I had dressed well—my tie was an embellishment, an effort not many would make. I had practised and put careful consideration into the songs; I felt I knew them from the inside. How much better could the others have done? If she was seeing three or four others, I should have been close to the top.

I saw the old woman again, knowing her immediately because of the scarves. She had given up on the bus too. She was walking ahead with two heavy bags, one in each hand, stooped and seeming even smaller now on the sidewalk. I had deliberately ignored her earlier, on the bus, and remembering that, I was ashamed to see her again. Her expression had been lonely and tired when I first saw her—I didn't want to pity her, or imagine her small life; I had wanted to go to my audition optimistic and light. Maybe her husband had died, or she couldn't drive or afford to keep a car, maybe her children had moved far away. Maybe all those things. And I had looked away from her life, finding it ugly: what a meaningless little selfishness.

I felt an impulse—like running in the tunnel beside the train—I could run up to her and offer to carry a bag. But it would terrify her. I was a stranger; she wouldn't remember me from the bus, or perhaps it would be worse if she did.

I paused, caught in the idea. I could offer to help. I played it out in my mind—if she was uncomfortable, I would leave. I could do it.

A moment passed. I didn't do it. She turned up a street and out of sight.

Late-day November sun was already lowering in the sky, and the light was heavier, golder now. As I walked home, I glanced inside shops and restaurants, catching snippets of the lives inside. People lined up at a counter, a bookstore with two women chatting, a family hunched in tight fast-food tables. A man on a bicycle passed me, pulling himself heavily along, his pants, flecked with mud and slush, tucked into worker's boots. I passed strings of children following their mothers. I felt everyone was good and everything was right. It was everywhere in my body— heart, bowels, knees, muscles criss-crossing my legs, sensitive lungs filled with light. Gratitude, and a sudden tenderness, instead of blood.

I lived above a small shawarma restaurant, a long and narrow space. Ibrahim's Grill was new and done entirely in white—walls, tables, and chairs. The owner had hung large colour images of the meals throughout the restaurant, as well as one photograph of a small, dusty, yellow-brick apartment with potted flowers hanging in the windows.

Back home? The food was good; you could get a dinner plate heavy with meat and rice, criss-crossed with lines of sauce, and it was not expensive. But the restaurant was new, it wasn't busy yet. I opened my street-level door and went up the stairs to my place.

Inside was warm. Light poured into my west-facing apartment. It was a small place crowded with shelves stacked high with books and music and movies, and I had managed to keep a massive palm plant for three years now—it was like having a shaggy, mute friend in the room. The other friend in here was a worn, brown corduroy couch, going bald on the arms. I had never known how much I needed a corduroy couch until I was in the thrift store and I saw a big brown thing against the wall, lumpy and ignored by the rest of the world. And at home it was like another person in the room: friendly, grateful, and a little old.

I hung my coat by the door and set my case down on the table where I sometimes ate, but where I mostly put mail and flyers and random papers. I wanted to tend to my shoes first. I untied them and pulled them off, brought them to the kitchen, dampened a paper towel and wiped the street salt from the black leather. I dabbed them dry with a dish towel and put them in a closet in the hall. I opened the trumpet case and looked at it for a minute, feeling relief and gratitude again—it was over. I emptied the water keys over the sink, then sat down at the table to wipe down the instrument. I cleaned the mouthpiece and put it back in the case. I looked at the trumpet again, sitting there in the open case.

I had lied to Lucia. "This is all I do." As if I was some kind of trumpet savant, my identity twisted up in the metal—the artist who exists for their art, suffering for their tormenting muse; their expression and freedom, their self pouring through the instrument. Actually, I did not doubt that was true for some, but I knew it was not true for me.

I had lied to Lucia because I did this mostly for money, and I did not enjoy auditions, and I resented having to try so hard for it. Suffering in front of strangers, going to the bathroom and looking at myself in the mirror, not recognizing that face, feeling strange to myself. Too many gigs were disappointing. I had done weddings and corporate events, one music video shoot where I fake-played in the background, and random one-offs when the usual player was unavailable. I had helped a few small local bands and one pianist record in studio—I had enjoyed that. But pay was low and the songs were middling.

I only ever had one long-term gig, playing a few nights a week at a steak house downtown where the bill at each table was more than I was making that night. Then the economy tumbled and all those rich guys stopped going out for steak, so they cancelled the band. I assume those guys were still rich out there somewhere—they were just eating less steak. It was an odd choice anyway, live music in that steak house. I don't think those guys cared.

Playing with a band—trusting them, understanding them—and being present with a song, it felt good and right. But repetition did not suit me. And if I did not like a song, playing it forty times was not going to improve the sentiment. Regular gigs were hard to get anyway; Salottino was only a seasonal spot. I had spent years on the leftovers. I didn't write anything myself. There was no fame or money to pursue. I could tuck away my trumpet for weeks if there was no reason to play; I wasn't driven toward it, I wasn't obsessed. I didn't dream about it or talk about it. It was just something I had done for a long time. Starting with my grandmother in that kitchen—and then years of repetition.

Finding some kind of beauty in it was rare; I could almost only find it alone. Like a loose thread left over from somewhere else, it was something small for me.

I closed the case and put it on a small desk in the corner of the room. I sat on the couch, falling deep into the cushions; the light was gauzy in the room and, outside, the sky was luminous in pink. Perhaps I hadn't truly lied to her. "All I do"—perhaps it was that, in a way. I didn't do much else. The trumpet did not call to me, but I had no other calling. Let her think it was the most important thing about me, rather than knowing I had no important things. I was a guy standing at the back, listening to a Stones song, or Otis or Amy, knowing there was something beautiful there—but knowing it was not mine.

EARLY OCTOBER

WHEN THEY PULL you into a room like this, you already know.

"Anastasia," Ruth said, smiling.

I had been summoned by Anita, and when she said the larger meeting room, I sensed it, a quietly moving doom, one I had suspected but not believed for a while. And when I went in and saw Ruth from HR already there—a stout, friendly woman with almost zero human intelligence—I knew for sure. I wasn't getting it.

Anita followed me in and sat down next to Ruth. "Anastasia—I keep forgetting that's your full name," Ruth said, closing a slim folder. Still, she was smiling. As always, she looked like a short turtle with an undersized head.

"Yes, it's a lot of weight to put on a little kid's shoulders, so I used Stasia when I was growing up, or just Stasi. Never went back." I was patient; I had two or three conversations with Ruth per year, mostly in the kitchen and always unintentional, usually about weather changes. I took care to pronounce the "s" differently in "Stasi" to avoid the East German thing; most people in my professional life used Stasia anyway. Anastasia—five syllables, a name with a tiered gown, a cold, aloof queen. Heavy is the head, et cetera. A ludicrous name in most experiences of daily human life.

I had never liked this room. It was a little bit too narrow for the table they had purchased for it, so you had to shuffle around, somewhat restrained by the chairs along the long side, almost sidestepping, to get to your seat, about six chairs later. I had noticed Anita struggling, bumping into two chairs as she got around to her side of the table, next to Ruth. It was just a dumb omission. Someone had ordered a wide table without measuring the width of the room, without measuring chair depth and the clearance needed behind; it was the sort of thing one might call "thoughtless," as if it was harmless, when the truth was thoughtless people did harmful things all the time—intent was not the most important thing—and those people should be removed from decision-making positions. Making decisions is hard work, or at least it should be. The fat chairs in the room were in beige leather—unsettling, it looked like skin—so the chairs sat around the too-big table like fat, headless bodies, turned this way and that. Whoever bought them didn't even think to get the swivel-return on the mechanism. I often found myself distracted and unsettled in this room, looking at the headless bodies—although that accurately described a lot of meetings here.

Anita started talking about the VP position and the reasoning behind the role, and Ruth chimed in, but I already knew they were giving it to Sara. I had seen her coming in two days ago, and I had ignored that with immense will.

Anita was uneasy talking, Ruth was nodding between us, I was watching without listening. When I looked at Anita, she also looked like a turtle—it was a gift Christopher had given me, saying that pretty much everyone looked like a turtle, you just had to take a moment to see them that way. Looking at Anita I saw how she was a thin-necked and hollow-chested turtle with prominent cheekbones and round glasses. An absolute turtle. But it wasn't amusing now. They were segueing into the part about me not getting the VP job and I was getting restless so I lifted up my palms and they both stopped talking, eyes flicking wide.

"Listen," I said. "I know I didn't get it. I disagree with the decision but I accept the decision, and we don't need to talk about it."

Both faces were startled, as if their next footstep had been pulled out. Ruth's mouth sat slightly open, even though she hadn't been talking. I kept going.

"It's OK, I knew it might happen, I wouldn't get the job."

I thought they would argue their right to keep to their prepared remarks, none of which I would agree with, and I wanted to cut them off completely. Remove the whole limb.

"And I'm fine with it." I broke the words off, dry.

We already knew Sara through a corporate partnership from a couple years back and we saw her regularly. And I knew why she got it. Calm, polished, blue-blooded, diplomatic, a mediocre track record from a much bigger company—it was ludicrous to me and having them attempt to rationalize it with logic or factual information would be like watching two turtles struggling feebly on their backs, kicking at the air. Sara was a showpiece for the company. What's done is done; I didn't want to talk about it. I wanted a cigarette.

Ruth was blank, lips apart. Anita handled it better, pivoting. "I know you've been with the company a long time, since almost the beginning," she said.

Now she was going to acknowledge my feelings and validate them. But I wanted the cigarette, not the emotional intelligence. "That's true, but I understand the decision—you do what you have to do." I started to rise from my seat. Ruth's eyes panicked but I smiled at her, and then at Anita, very reassuring, very soothing, a skill I had acquired in sales, so they knew I wanted to move past it quickly. The last thing we should all be doing was rolling around in this. I stood up. I only had to move around slightly less than half the table length to reach the door, but they were stuck on the other side, so they'd have to shuffle around. Not bad, actually.

"OK, Stasia," Anita said, starting to rise as well. "Well, thanks for understanding."

"No problem, Anita," I said. She was VP Operations for less than two years. Like Sara, she came from somewhere big and bland.

"Thanks, Stasia," Ruth said. HR Director for three.

"Of course, Ruth," I said.

I got out of the room and returned to my desk and collected my wallet and keys and phone. I slipped out of the office and got into my car and drove to the store where I bought a pack of cigarettes—my first in about eight or nine months, in a nine-year attempt to quit—and unwrapped them in the car. I tapped the pack lightly, thinking. I could text instead. But that would be a whole session, an urgent back-and-forth that would last half an hour. It seemed like a lot of work, a lot of comforting. And I would be doing the comforting. I took a lighter from the glove compartment, lit up, and took a nice pull, opening the window mid-haul as I realized I would be exhaling soon, then suddenly re-membering I had forgotten my coat at the office. With the window open I would get cold; I was only in my blazer. Still, it was a wool blazer, a thick wool, tight-knit and warm. I exhaled out the window.

I wasn't even angry yet. Acquiring the cigarette and then smoking four in a row was honestly all I wanted to feel, both edgy and soothed—I might as well feel instead of think right now, exhaust my sensitivity that way. The fa-miliar bitterness of smoking was a sharp-edged thing to do to my body. I also decided to get the chicken shawarma on my way home, not the falafel, and I would eat that in the car too; I was supposed to be a vegetarian.

Much of the afternoon was a blur, but I left a little early and played out the conversation with Christopher on the drive home. I got off the highway early and cruised slowly through smaller streets. He would be upset, but if I remained calm he would also remain calm. Same with Sarah, my daughter.

I could, at the soonest, get angry on the weekend, if I had the time and could spend it alone. I considered it briefly. No Mateo either.

Pulling into the driveway, I didn't get out right away. The evening blue was growing deeper and the headlights blared white circles on the garage door—I cut the lights. I drew another cigarette from the pack and smoked it slowly, thoughtfully. If I lowered the seat I could see a part of my face in the side mirror, an attractive part of my face, catch-ing the lines around my mouth when I took a drag. It was that wincing expression that smokers recognize, the mask, the self-imposed distance from everyone.

The sky was dimming outside but, with the window open, I watched the circle of my face in the side mirror, the pulls, the exhalations, the briefly obscuring smoke. In the late light, I recognized myself.

***

Christopher had been cautious after I told him about it, picking his way around me like a careful deer. But we would be okay—I had already decided I wasn't going to punish him with moods or silences.

I had, however, gone into the yard with the shears and chopped off all the roses' heads, every single one. I brought them inside and arranged them in wooden and glass bowls for the kitchen island and living room. Sarah was deeply struck by them, the exquisite elaborations of their shape in their sudden new form. A pile of rose heads, beauty unfailing. But for me it was bloodlust. Slashing their heads clean from their stems was near-sexual—over and over and over and over. Each chop got better, climbing from the creamy satisfaction of the previous. Over and over. Christopher had looked down at the piles of heads in bowls. "I am thinking about trying therapy," I said to him. Our eyes had locked for two or three seconds, then we both grinned—in terms of me acting out, that was more or less it.

I was sitting on Isabelle's loveseat, looking around the room, thinking about those roses. There were several plump pillows around me in friendly colours with soothing, wavy lines.

The room had a lot of natural light—lucky. It was grounding. In the light of day—that saying, it means you can lose track of what's happening, you can lose yourself in monotony or chaos, and the light of day brings you back, shows it plainly. So here we were now, in the light of day.

The walls were painted deep taupe and cluttered with nature pictures and framed certificates and diplomas, some of which I suspected were less than wall-worthy, but clearly this was the dominance display. It was interesting, posting all your accomplishments to face people who were facing you. Other professions did this too, mostly the ones that charge by the hour. It makes sense for her; psychology is the specialty and she knows this psychological play will catch 90 per cent of people. But for the remaining 10 per cent, they must know this looks bad. Showing off always shows a weakness, somewhere near the core.

"Welcome, Anastasia," she said, "I'm glad you've come."

"Yes, thanks—but I go by Stasia. Or Stasi." I had put that on the form. Either she didn't read it or didn't remember.

"Of course, that's right," Isabelle said, unblinking. "Stasia, of course."

"It's good to be here too," I said.

It did not improve much from there. The first session we just covered why I was there more immediately—the VP job—and then started on childhood a bit. And then the fifty minutes were over and it was time to leave, to turn off the emotional tap I had opened for the benefit of her understanding, for which I was, of course, paying. And then the tap was sharply closed. Just go home to your family and go to bed, see you next week, we'll do this thing again.

They should have therapy retreats where you just talk yourself to exhaustion—no more time limits, no clocks—and by the time you're finished, you're done. However many hours it takes—eight, twenty, forty-five. Done, cured, over it. You spend such a continuous and cumulative amount of time labouring and describing and complaining that you end up processing it all and you just stop caring.

It would be the exhaustion that brings you home, resting finally into a body and mind no longer at war with its various selves. Just tired of thinking about yourself. In a truly simple, childlike way. Reborn. In reality it might be illegal somehow, but I did consider such a business model and how much you could charge, and wondered what the relapse rates might look like.

I returned for another session, now in a few hundred dollars deep. We finished my childhood and started chipping away at adulthood. And of course we stumbled into him. Unsurprisingly, Mateo took centre stage, and a lot of her questions focused on him. I'd only known Mateo for a couple years now; I had almost forty years of other selves. But Mateo was going to be the delicious part for her, it was going to be full of meaning, I could tell.

"Who pursued whom?" she asked.

"I don't remember, it was vague," I said.

"So how did it come together?"

I told her—a pretty ordinary story actually, which of course it did not seem at the time. At the time I thought it was the only available reality giving oxygen and light. But it started with in-person interactions and then moved to social media and then we got burner phones. I guess we recognized urgency in the other. That was it; I couldn't tell if it was more me or more him.

"What do you think it gave to you?"

"Gave to me?"

"Added to your life."

I remember the months of waiting. After seeing each other, months of sizing up and confirming what we each wanted to know, like two threats recognizing each other in the street, circling, deciding what kind of damage could be done. I saw it in his face when I first met him, his bored, slack eyes suddenly tightening into focus, an arrogance rising. He was too arrogant to marry, could not find a woman to match him and own him, but of course he lived with a woman for a long time; I imagine she accepted him hungrily, took care of him, made him meals, all that. A sturdy and simple female for sleeping and eating. He needed her but resented it, because that was his way—to resent what was closest to him. He had that brazen impulse to wrestle free, to bite the hands that held him, to scan the horizon for new movement, to chase. In that way, he had separated his fire and his earth. And that was my story as well; neither of us had learned how to live with one only, too arrogant and reckless, too willing to hurt.

I thought this way at least most of the time, but not always. Sometimes I had a vague confusion about Mateo, a disorientation, as if he were a portrait out of focus; he would throw bewildering flares that were out of character, act out, before falling back to normal, before taking his rest. And I never knew what they meant. But reality would return to us, reliable and crisp.

I did remember that time, as we circled each other—such a long stretch of light collecting throughout the day that I would savour into the evening. Light, but also air—ever-present and invisible, something very close to survival as everything else drained of meaning. Including Sarah, including Christopher. I remember what it did to my body, suddenly alive, darkly silent, a kind of madness at the edge of instinct. Losing my balance for the first time in my life, I had tipped and fallen in.

"Have you done this before?" she asked.

"No," I said.

She stopped and took a minute writing on her notepad, letting silence fall between us, and leaving it there. I let her write, and looked out the window.

Strange that it had happened now in my life; I had denied myself many times before and never felt poorer for it. I had married Christopher for the same reasons I remained married to him—he had had a good childhood. He was whole. It was a thoughtless cliché, what I was doing, tediously middle-class and middle-age, and I resented having to explore that with her—her with all the framed papers on the wall, as if she possessed perfect knowledge of us flailing, weeping mortals. It was humiliating to both of us to pretend this was important, because these were only the details of life, only the trimmings, and they would never matter until I understood what it meant to be alive—bruisingly, painfully alive. Enough about Mateo already.

Outside her window there was a tree.

"So why Mateo, then? And why now?"

Behind the tree, there were other trees, thinner and younger, bending bare limbs in the moving air. We were going to spend the rest of the session on him—I predicted that, but it still stung, a sexist thing in my mind. A man could do this and it would be but one aspect of him; when a woman does it, betrays her family, it's every thing and all things. Actually, I didn't really know if Isabelle thought that—it was a slant I was sensitive to; I might have said it to myself. Outside the window, behind the trees, I could see the edge of a road. Every few seconds a car moved across it before disappearing from sight. There weren't many interesting answers to her questions, I felt my words mocking me shortly after leaving my mouth, truthful little children betraying.

"I'm not sure why," I said. "He was in the same place as me. We recognized each other."

Which insight was she expecting? She would know the reasons already, maybe one of those certificates were about it. Which one should I say—thrill seeking? Novelty? So much of my body and blood had been purposed for acquiring sex and it was not properly reassigned later in life? Boredom? Something about monogamy? Something delicate and precious about my childhood? Vague trauma? Anger? No, anger is for the young—bitterness? Trying to wake up things I knew were dead? And my smug suspicion—that so many of us were wordlessly dead but refusing to join them, to sleep like that, to rest until my body fell away like leaves rustling and gone. Pick any of the reasons, mix them up, roll them out. See what's facing up.

Sometimes the movement of the cars outside was rhythmic, regular, a bright colour ticking by, then another, then another. Sometimes the cars streamed by rapidly one after the other—red, black, black, white, blue, beige. I had not been treating Sarah well at home since they told me—it was an inconvenient detail to Isabelle, and everybody else, that Sara at work had the same name as Sarah my daughter. When I snapped the name at home, its weight had doubled. Sarah knew I'd missed a job I had earned for a long time, and sometimes she watched me quietly from across the room; I didn't know what she saw. At seven, she was already a watchful, sensitive child—our bloodline. An unbroken chain, even when we bred outside the temperament. It would not be diminished, it loomed above every secondary trait—we were sensitive to every pattern, texture, tremor, every warmth and coolness of life. It was our call, more vibration than sound, felt only by a few.

"And what do you think it gave him?"

"I have no idea. A break, a change."

Isabelle was not as interested in my younger brother, Peter. Distant and sensitive, I had spent so much time when we were children protecting Peter. He played the trumpet but never bothered to write his own music, although I heard him fiddling around and, suspended for a moment, I would wait for the next note, and the next one, and the next one. It was like hearing someone speak at last. He was lazy and loose with it, but he was saying something, in his mellow golden way. But he didn't pursue it. Peter wasn't a fighter, he wasn't going to fight through unpleasant things to earn his own place. Anything he had I had fought for on his behalf. I got him the job at the restaurant, I found his apartment through a friend. I sent him articles about highly sensitive people, HSPs, because I saw it in us and I hoped it would help him see himself. I lent him money and stood up for him and never asked him for what I wanted—an equal, not another person who needed my care.

Isabelle and I had spent some time on my mother, the twenty-year snapshot of me living at home with her: the undiagnosed agoraphobe, panic disorder, unmedicated for almost all those years, abandoned in divorce while nearly disabled, unable to handle busy intersections or remain calm in grocery stores, running out, hiding in the car, leaving me with a full cart, facing alarmed cashiers at checkout. I was sixteen, I was thirteen, I was eleven. My father remarried, moving to Europe and making up for lost time by hiking through calm, snow-tipped mountains and navigating frothy rapids. He posted his adventures a lot. He married someone petite, active, tenacious, grabbing the world's natural beauty by the throat and strangling the meaning out of it. Fair enough. We all had our things. I ran half marathons and fucked another man. With nourishing self-loathing, I might add—my renewable resource, and the inevitable snapback of arrogance against it; I already knew I was stronger and smarter than almost everybody else. If anything, the self-loathing humbled me just enough to stay engaged with the world.

"So you don't talk about it," Isabelle said. She was still on Mateo.

"Why he's doing it? No. I don't ask."

I had a cigarette in the car. It was a mild, pale evening. The fifty minutes had ended as abruptly as before, snapping off something I had been nursing open. Maybe this was the best way to do it, maybe they did studies, perhaps the increments held mysterious benefits of learning how to open and close the strong, unknown currents with a stranger. I was willing to be wrong.

On my way home

Christopher would be waiting to hear that and then he would put the tray in the oven. Sarah would look up at the sound of the phone. But I had time. You can say traffic or whatever.

I lit a second cigarette and opened my big bag, rummaging to the bottom, feeling along the edge where there was a slit in the lining. I slipped my hand inside the hole and felt around, deep into the left, deep into the right, far back; finally my fingers brushed against the phone. I pulled it out and turned it on. It booted up, slowly, running through its starting screens; I waited to see if any message would arrive. Nothing. I waited an extra minute, smoking. Still nothing. As always. But life was like this: checking, checking. Me alone with a phone, checking.

I was almost done the cigarette; I picked a heart—the smaller, humble one—and sent it. I turned off the phone and slipped it into the bottom of the bag, inside the lining, pushing it back. I leaned back into my seat and finished the cigarette, refusing to let myself fall into calculations of what the text was and how it would be received.

The drive home was unmemorable. The checking was behind me; I would sleep well. It was dark outside, cooling into autumn but not yet hardening for winter. The fall trees were beautiful, though—turning leaves, sudden new colour, and the slim few that were already bare. I liked both, the tousled red-golds, the sombre nudes.

TUESDAY

IT HAD RAINED in the morning, the damp air warming slightly as a soft mist retreated. The last remnants of ice had washed off the wet sidewalk. There was no sun; the sky stretched end to end in unbroken grey. I was starting work at eleven—on a grey day, or a cold day, it was nice coming into a kitchen. With the audition behind me, I still felt the lightness of relief, having the day to work with my hands, turning it over in my mind.

Stu worked prep and grill full-time, and I knew him to be moody and thin-skinned. I came in and said hello and he nodded, unsmiling, not looking at me. I sensed a cool mood and I knew about those; it was best to leave him alone. Stu hated if you were perky and tried to bring him out of it. I went through to the back and hung up my coat. I looked at the schedule, still written by hand, to see who else was in—it was the regular Tuesday lineup.

Tuesdays had been different for me for the past six or seven months. The owner wanted to make little cream-puff pastries for afternoon takeout and for dinner crowds—basically profiteroles, but with a slightly oblong shape—because we had no in-house dessert otherwise, and they packed well to go. They weren't cheap to make, but we could charge a good price for the presentation, their charming shapes and the little surprise of cream inside. I removed my watch and put it in my pocket, washed my hands with dish soap at the big sink. We had a room of sixteen tables and almost half our business was takeout. We did deluxe sandwiches, salads and thick-cut fries, and three pasta dishes, and we served wine and beer. Marc, the owner—the only child of the couple who opened the place when it was three times the size and a proper French restaurant—wanted us to start making cream puffs from his parents' recipe. We only had the dozen-odd tables, but sometimes people wanted something sweet after a meal, even lunch, he said. And they travelled well in a box. I went into the cooler for butter and milk and eggs, passing Stu, who was still silent.

The pastries were selling well. We had a few regular customers early on. An office manager from the building across the street bought a dozen every Monday for a weekly meeting. A big burly guy who didn't talk much got a dozen almost every week, and we never knew if he was a business owner somewhere in the area, or a family man, or if he just ate them all himself. And a nearby florist, Indira, a petite and chatty woman, got some for her staff. Those were the regulars. I took a large sack of flour from the cupboard and the big five-cup measure. I set the oven.

So Tuesdays I made the shells, when it was quieter in the kitchen. Usually close to 120 of them, as much as the dough would last. And I made the cream and piped in the first forty, stored the rest of the cream, froze the rest of the shells. They would be tended to throughout the week. They were smallish. Our serving was two per plate, but for takeout people could order any number. We infused the cream with a bit of lemon, coated the tops with a lick of sweet ginger glaze and a pinch of coconut flakes. Very small amounts—hints. You weren't necessarily supposed to know it was ginger, or taste the lemon. The filling was supposed to have its own flavour without you recognizing the individual parts—Marc's parents had specified that. And it didn't taste quite like anything else. It was both bright and creamy, light and rich. My batch would usually last through Friday night. Arlin, an easy-going part-time guy I liked, made another batch on Saturday mornings; they disappeared over the weekend.

Stu was pulling out small thawed steaks and cutting them out of their packs. He worked quickly, his eyes on his hands, following the quick movement of the knife. I didn't think our steak sandwich was very good. The toppings were okay but the cut was too tough. It didn't sell well.

Stu was smooth with the blade, tossing the steaks aside. He was a tall guy with a lean face, partially covered with an erratic beard. His long forearms were striped with black hair; his skin was otherwise very pale. He was lanky, like a runner, save for the small pot-belly hanging from his narrow frame. He didn't eat well. He had dropped out of college, and the reasons seemed to change based on his mood. I put water, butter, and salt into a large pot and set the temperature high. And he played a lot of video games.

"You weren't here yesterday," Stu said without looking across at me. He was still cutting steaks out of packs, with regular swipes. It wasn't phrased as a question, but he was asking.

"Yeah, I had that audition," I said. I started to measure out the flour.

"Oh right," he said, glancing up.

Ange came to the back with stacked plates and cutlery. "Oh hey, Peter," she said, light and chirpy. Ange was all high-speed smiles, short and stout, her walk a happy wiggle like she had a swivel in her spine right at the waist. Friendly to everybody in the exact same way, so that you felt you didn't know her at all. She came from Haiti about a decade ago and spoke immaculately dainty French, which delighted her tables. Never saw her in a bad mood once, exceptional at ignoring unpleasant customers—probably a perfect server.

"Hey, Ange," I said. She dunked the dishes and smiled at me and swivelled out.

I took the eggs out of the cartons and lined them up carefully, redirecting them when they tried to roll in some other direction, escape their small round fates.

"I forgot about the audition, how did it go?" Stu asked. His mood was brighter already.

I guessed he had been annoyed the day before when I didn't come in and he didn't know why. I imagined he suspected I was doing something more interesting than kitchen prep and he was resentful. Stu seemed annoyed when other people left the job to go somewhere else, or when people were in school and then graduated and got whatever jobs they had been training for. He didn't like any of those people. Leaving this behind—showing they could, and they wanted to. But Stu knew I was sticking around. He knew a trumpet was nothing.

"It went great," I said. "I did three songs. 'Crimson and Clover.' One by the Stones. And a Christmas one."

"What was the Christmas one?"

"'White Christmas.'"

"Of course," Stu said.

A few tiny bubbles clung to the bottom of the big pot, but no real bubbles yet. I turned some of the eggs around and let them go gently. They turned slowly in soft, uneven ways.

"Do you think you'll get it?" Stu asked.

"Maybe. It really depends who else they asked." I leaned down on the steel prep counter. I turned a few more eggs, watching them.

Stu was really into the topic now. "Where is it? How many nights a week?"

I knew he didn't really talk to anyone else here. Hassan, who took my shift yesterday—Stu wouldn't say his sarcastic things to him, he wouldn't make fun of Marc, he wouldn't describe customers he thought were stupid. Or fat—Stu especially hated fat people. He hated everybody somewhat but reserved extra emphasis for the obese. It was a segment of people he finally felt fully superior to, yet that wasn't enough to make him gentle.

"Friday and Saturday nights, this Mediterranean place in the west end. Salottino. And I know the drummer from before."

"Oh yeah? He put in a good word?"

"Maybe, I don't ask that stuff," I said. I didn't say the band wasn't there.

"Salottino, I think I've been there."

I knew he had not. But this was Stu, trying. I checked my water, still not boiling—but close. I didn't respond.

"Still, you should ask the drummer to say something," Stu said.

I didn't say anything and walked back to the posted schedule, reading it over again. I had already seen it, but I wanted to break the topic with Stu. Elijah was the other server today, a smooth and gorgeous college student. He was studying finance but also had a modelling agent and apparently filmed online spots once in a while. But I don't think he cared for it so much—his tips were extraordinary and he seemed to really want to be a financial adviser. He said he wanted to join a big company and have an office and whatever new Audi sports car they were making in five years. I knew he would get what he wanted. I could imagine him with an equally gorgeous and smooth partner, an open relationship, of course, with no fits of jealousy or insecurity, no mess, no complications—both of them blissful recipients of every easy beauty and clean pleasure in the world.

Stu was wrapping up the steak prep. I came back to my boiling water. I dropped the heat and dumped in heavy cups of flour. Elijah came to the back.

"Peter!" he said. "Missed you yesterday."

"Hey, Elijah."

He dumped his dishes in the sink. Stu went into the cooler and closed the door behind him. He didn't like Elijah. Elijah probably had five or six different things he could do with his life, quite successfully. He was equanimous, good-looking, healthy inside and out—unperturbed by other people. Liked by both men and women. Another perfect server. I don't know how Marc found them, but he was good at keeping them. Elijah didn't ask where I had been; he grinned at me and went back out. Bye, Elijah.

I stirred the heavy dough that was forming, and Stu came out of the cooler. "Missed you yesterday," he repeated. I gave a wry smile into the pot so he would think his joke landed, but I didn't care. I liked Elijah enough. The dough was sticking and releasing from the sides of the pot as I went around and around. Elijah would finish college and run off to real life. I didn't envy him, I didn't want that for myself. College seemed another series of small auditions, but for me to finance with years of debt. Pass.

I started introducing eggs and mixing. I thought about Lucia, in a kitchen in the west end of the city, a big kitchen, a chef who had studied somewhere, her suppliers coming in and out with thousand-dollar invoices. Reservations steadily collecting. A serious woman running a significant restaurant, born into it but without that second-generation insolence. Sometimes I thought Marc was lacking that humility—he was fair with staff, but he was given a restaurant by his parents and was often flippant about it. Hard done by, in his mind, by the tedium. Yet he never said what it was he wanted instead. I knew Lucia less than an hour and I knew she was not like that.

Stu was focusing more on grill now, helping Sadil. Our takeout counter under the lamps was slowly collecting containers. It was getting busier, but still just a Tuesday variation of busy, which was not much. I was balling and stretching dough and putting trays in the oven—it was a smaller oven, I would spend significant portions of my afternoon rotating, clearing, and refilling baking trays with a relentless timer. That timer—after a baking shift, I sometimes heard it in my dreams, not always the actual sound but how the sound felt, even the expectant silence before it started. But it was a good break from Stu, who was getting chatty and would likely remain so for the rest of the day. He was silent on grill, not talking to Sadil, not taking much interest in a man who had a different background and was a different age than him.

I remember the day when it occurred to me that I spent more time with Stu than any other person. That was a blank, overcast moment. I was here eight years and Stu was here the whole time—longer than me—and I would never have picked him to spend so much of my life with. Jobs were like that. Not just where you went every day, and money, and identity—if it meant something to you, or had status—but determining who you spent all your time with. You can't pick your family, but as you grow up, you can manoeuvre around, live through choices. I didn't intend to make a long series of choices that brought me to Stu. Spending almost every day with him and his mercurial highs and lows.

He just tired me out. He seemed to hate most people, yet he was astonishingly sensitive in every regard, and I struggled to understand that, let alone see it as a cause. It was a mistake to think sensitive people would always be kind. I think you'd find sensitive people among the most angry, most bitterly closed. They spent years protecting themselves from careless remarks and an ugly, grasping world—they grew defensive. The shell grew too thick. I got along with Stu because I learned how to; I was non-threatening. I did my job, which overlapped with his, and I didn't talk a lot. I think I passed under his radar, sensitively tuned to threats. I don't think I was ever important enough.

The only thing I was sure of in Stu's life was that someone, from a very young age, had beat the shit out of him. Regularly, and with malice. Emotionally maybe. Could have been his mother, an obese woman he mocked with disgust in the rare moments he mentioned her. Or maybe some stepfather, some older man. Or kids at school. Whoever it had been, a little boy named Stuart was bruised and broken and long forgotten. I was sure of it. But he never said anything.

The way I rotated trays in our small oven, the timer was going off every six or eight minutes. Stu came to the back. "Sadil's an idiot," he said to me. "Been here like nine months and still ruining the grilled peppers." He went into the cooler and brought out a container of sliced red peppers, softened in vinaigrette. "I'll have to prep more tomorrow, probably." He used tongs to drag a large clump into a serving bowl. "Marc doesn't care anyway. He's not the one who has to deal with it." He left. In terms of one-minute increments of Stu, it was immaculate.

Elijah was back a moment later. "Hey, Peter. How are those puffs?"

"Good, good." I was stirring cold whipped cream, leftovers I hoped to use, but it was mostly collapsing now.

Elijah paused, remembering. "Oh wait, did you have a thing yesterday?"

"Yeah. I had an audition."

"Audition—great. Where did you go?"

"A restaurant in the west end, Salottino's. Two nights a week for the winter. Their regular guy is coming back in February or March."

"That's great, Peter," Elijah said. "I bet you get it."

"Yeah, maybe," I said. I stopped stirring the cream for a moment. "Oh hey, I'm going out tomorrow night. Can we do the regular? Forty?"

"Of course," he said, suddenly breaking into his liquid grin. "Little extra for you, this time. Bathroom in three."

Elijah got something from his coat, and then went into the bathroom. I scraped the bulk of the cream into the garbage;

it would weigh down my new batch. I left some clinging to the sides, unimportant remnants, and got a carton of cream and two lemons from the cooler. I pulled out my wallet and took out two twenty-dollar bills, folding them neatly twice. Elijah was coming in through the back door, and I handed him the tidy folds as I passed him out the door. I went to the men's room, the stall on the left, and leaned down to the toilet paper dispenser on the wall. Tucked neatly into one corner was a bright white square. Maybe a bit thicker than usual. I put it into my pocket and came out of the stall, then through the back kitchen door. Elijah was already out front and Stu was just coming in. Sadil was following him. They separated as one went into the cooler and the other to the sink. And then, a moment later, Ange came in, smiling.

"Told me a woman he used to date had an accent like mine," she said, mostly to me, laughing. "Too much. And then fifty cents for tip. What a joke."

Everybody chatted up Ange and she was endlessly amused. She enjoyed telling the stories. She had a peach face—round, soft, and rosy—and could get anybody talking at a table. People asked her about the menu more than anyone else. Inevitably the chatter continued, encouraged by her scrunched nose and laughing eyes.

"You should've asked why she dumped him," I said. It was rare that I would say anything, let alone a soft joke. It went over pretty good.

Ange laughed, surprised, a big gleeful peal. "I need to ask more guys that," she said.

"Well." I smiled, shrugging.

"Hey, guys, Peter knows everything," she announced to the kitchen, which was Stu and Sadil getting different things and heading back out again without paying us attention.

"Peter knows it all." She was feeling generous, expansive with me. She was the type to delight in the shy ones, almost mothering. She turned and followed them out.

My timer was counting down. I liked Ange. I liked everybody enough, if I tilted my head and looked at it in the right way. But the best people were new people—like Lucia—wild expanses of unturned rocks, dark corners you were still trying to see.

I went back to the oven and readied myself for another round of rotations. I would finish preparing the cream during the next long stretch. Sometimes I wondered how much I had in common with Stu, how little I was different. Both sensitive but in opposite directions. Stu always kicking out at the world, me a struggling, blanking mute. Maybe a life with Stu was the natural result of a natural path, me ending up in a kitchen with a misanthrope. I wasn't a misanthrope, though—I just struggled to connect most of the time. With new people, even struggled to talk. I didn't dislike people, I just felt alone. But I wanted something better for myself—wasn't that the point—wanting something?

Marc came in. He was wearing that worn, ancient sheepskin coat that looked as if it had been very expensive fifteen or twenty years ago.

"Hey Peter," Marc said, "help with this?" He was carrying two canvas tote bags full of vegetables and large blocks of cheese. His face was pink from the cold outside.

"Yeah, sure." I took them from his arms and started emptying them on the counter, bringing the blocks into the cooler. The timer went off, a panicked bleating. I put on mitts and rotated the trays. I pulled off the mitts and started stripping and rinsing the vegetables in the sink. Marc had pulled off his coat and hung it, retreating into the back area where he had a makeshift office—a short desk pushed against the wall.

I broke the celery stalks down at the base and flushed out the grit. What an odd shape and taste, celery. These massive, hard, footlong stalks that we minced tiny or boiled soft to be able to ingest. Yet they were everywhere—celery was in every grocery store. Like it was some staple of life. I couldn't even imagine celery farmers eating it. Maybe that made sense, maybe you'd be tired of anything you grew. But celery especially—those farmers were making sandwiches with fat red tomatoes and stinging-sweet onions and curly green leaves. They weren't eating celery. Yet all of us participated in this idea—that this stringy, chewy, salted water fibre was somehow necessary—for what? Broth maybe. Get that salt out of those weird stalks.

Stu came back from the grill and dumped an empty bowl. "I'm not joking," he said. "He ruined two more peppers. He forgets them."

As a rule I didn't react to his bitching because, if I fed him, it would never end.

Looking down at me, Stu scrunched his nose. "I fucking hate celery."

And there it was. Stu had my anti-celery heart in his big, idiot hands. And he didn't even know.

I grinned down into the sink as I rubbed the ends of the stalks and got a container out for them. I had four eggplants next and a sack of potatoes. Our big order was weekly, but if we ran low on anything, Marc would pick up enough to tide us over.

Marc came out briefly, pulling lottery tickets out of his coat pocket, hanging near the door. "Oh hey," he said as he searched the bottoms of his inside pockets, "you had a thing yesterday."

"Audition, yeah," I said, turning eggplants gently in my hands under the water.

"How did it go?"

"Good, I think."

"A show, or?"

"Two nights a week at a res-restaurant—in the west end." I tripped over the words.

"Which one?"

"Salottino."

Marc's mouth and eyes flattened slightly. "Salottino? Yeah, I know it." He considered a memory for a moment. "Nice place." After another brief pause: "I didn't know they had live music."

"Maybe it's recent, I don't know. They had the ceilings done a long time ago. It's only two nights a week, maybe it depends what night you go."

"Right, yeah." Marc got the tickets out of his coat and ordered them briefly in his hands.

Ange and Elijah came to the back, each balancing a stack of dishes, each swinging the weight's centre with fluid confidence as they moved briskly around. Good servers always end up somewhere. It doesn't matter where they go after— they get it. People who've swung around crowded trays without looking at them, people who have served every kind of human without losing their inner quiet, they've figured something out, something the rest of us haven't. The blind physical awareness, the steadfast centre, the ease in every action performed, almost unaware—like when great musicians stop seeing the instrument.

"Peter, is something burning?" Ange looked at me, her brows pulled together.

She was right, something was—the air was sharper, suddenly catching in my throat. And I immediately knew. I had forgotten to set the timer after my last rotation, when

Marc came in. I yanked open the oven door and grey smoke poured out. I saw dark brown—blackened—domes of two trays with dozens of puffs. Ange was watching at first but went out again, disturbed.

"Shit," I said.

I grabbed the mitts and started pulling out the trays. Elijah stood and watched for a minute longer before returning out front. I put the burned trays on the counter and looked at them—neat rows of pale dough with hard, dark backs.

"Shit."

There were about three dozen of them, unsalvageable. I waved the remaining smoke away and reset the timer to make sure the other trays would move along. I should tell Marc. I didn't want to. It was a careless mistake, and he had picked me to work on these because I didn't often make careless mistakes.

I went to the back. Marc was at his desk with his lottery tickets out. He hadn't smelled the smoke yet. I hesitated. Every week or so he'd sit there with twenty or thirty tickets laid out all over the desk, in some kind of order, and he would start checking the numbers. Top to bottom. I didn't want to intrude. There was something hopeful and sad about the scene.

I stood there.

People who buy a lottery ticket here and there, okay. People who buy lots of lottery tickets all the time were really trying. I never knew what Marc wanted, and he never said. I guess he didn't want to work again. I looked at his back, the back of his head with its light brown waves, his round shoulders in a dark green sweater. He must have been in his late forties. He was lifting the tickets one at a time and checking the numbers with his phone.

"Marc," I said. "I burned a lot of puffs."

He put the ticket and his phone down and followed me.

We stood looking at them.

"Shit," he said.

"Yeah, I'm sorry. I missed setting the timer when you came in."

Marc was looking at them, nodding.

"I can make a small ball of dough and make up for it," I said. "Or if you think we can make it through Friday night about three dozen short."

"Let's make the dough," he said. "If we were running low, I wouldn't have anyone available on a Friday to work on them. I wouldn't want to run out."

"Okay, thanks, Marc. Sorry again about that."

"Yeah, no problem, it happens." He offered a small smile and went back to his desk and the tickets. He was fair, which I had expected.

Stu came to the back. "Shit," he said.

"Yeah." I was lifting and angling the tray to slide them off into the garbage. Most of them slid, a few rolled and tumbled. They made soft thunks at the bottom. "I forgot the timer."

"Turning into Sadil with the peppers." He swung into the cooler for a pop he kept there. He came out and took a drink from it, watching me prep the pot again, get everything out again, start measuring. Then he took out his phone and started scrolling. I already knew why he was bitter about Sadil—Sadil had once made a comment about some video game Stu had been playing. "My son plays that. He's thirteen. You still play games?"—something like that. Implying that Stu was a man doing a child's things, while Sadil was married with three kids, paying a mortgage. I was there; it was an offhand comment. And that was it. Stu would relish Sadil's failings forever, find pleasure in repeating them, have his victory at last. I checked on the pot, waiting for bubbles. The timer bleated and I rotated trays. Stu got bored and went back out to the grill again.

Kitchen prep was a luxury of wandering thoughts. Not like grill, where your mind cycled in ten-second loops—flip, stir, pull, what next, what's low?—a cleansing rhythm that had you operating fully in the moment, and shifts flying by. With prep, your hands could be busy but your mind was free. And I liked the time. I knew people who didn't like prep, got bored, but this suited me—I liked the time, I liked watching my hands work and being alone with my thoughts. I liked when my thoughts were not owned, not hired by something as mundane and constant as work.

Prep was how I had long stretches to think about Stu, wounded and mean, and later about my mom, her final and devastating sensitivity in a loud, abrupt world. Agoraphobic, a word I learned from Stasi; my mother had never said it. She was unmedicated for a long time, up until my twenties. She had made her world as small as possible—startled by noise and crowds, bruised by strangers—while Stu made his as solitary as possible by flinging out his disdain. Me, I was closer to my mother. But as I grew up, shy and sensitive, I saw how her life was curling in on itself, dying early and slowly. I didn't want to be like that. And Stasi, giving herself a warrior role, punching out into the world. More like Stu, she was easily hurt but turned that around with discipline, aloofness, sharp words.

I was stirring a small ball of dough around the pot, mashing it into the sides, then pulling it away. It was not something anyone had shown me, but I figured it couldn't hurt, and it looked good.

People like Elijah and Ange—fundamentally insensitive, but not unkind—nothing bothered them. They could glide through life's inconveniences and disappointments; it never made them cruel, or hesitant, or fearful. It was easy to envy them, but I also knew it was not a way I wanted to go through my own life, almost without perception, untouched by anything. But I marvelled nonetheless.

The timer beeped. I put on gloves, opened the oven door, and rotated trays. I also thought about Marc sometimes—couldn't figure that guy out. Easygoing, good with the staff, fair and accommodating. But this thing with the lottery tickets, I couldn't tell if it made me sad because he would never win, or because he was trying desperately to escape something. Some people talked about winning the lottery for this right here—having your own little business, running something yourself, a colourful café, a small wine bar on the corner, a bookstore. Marc had that already and kept buying dozens of tickets for his escape to something he never talked about. It confused and alarmed me because I didn't otherwise see a reason to pity him. And then this piteous thing.

Stu came to the back again. He watched me for a few minutes without saying anything. I was moving some of the pastries onto a rack. "Hey, I'll help," he said.

"Nah, you don't have to."

"No problem, I've seen you do it." He prepped a tray and scooped the dough ball into the pastry bag. He piped a few of them out.

"Not bad, Stu," I said. He was pleased with himself, pleased with my assessment. "You can be my understudy," I added.

"Hah, right, a kid like you." Stu wasn't much older than me but he liked to joke like that, sound more mature, more of a man. I reset the timer.

"Aww, guys." Marc came out of his office and was heading out front, turning to mock us. "Teamwork—you guys are so cute."

"Peter was burning them," Stu said.

Marc liked that and he grinned over his shoulder as he passed.

Stu was feeling upbeat. He didn't usually joke with Marc—didn't like him, obviously, though I never knew why. Probably something small and dumb.

"Okay," I said, "you're taking my job. Go help Sadil on grill."

"It's quiet," Stu said. "And I can't help Sadil. No one can help that guy."

"He's not that bad—you're just being Stu."

He smirked. "I'm always Stu. But he's wrecking the peppers."

"You don't care about peppers." I wanted him gone, but I had to keep the friendly tone. "Get out of here, eh? I'll burn them again if you distract me." I took the pastry bag from him and started to pipe out the rest.

Stu went into the cooler, got his pop, then went out to the grill again. He didn't seem put off but I wouldn't have minded if he sulked, either: I could be alone with my thoughts again. And he would forgive me, I was forgivable to him. The tray was done, I could start whipping the fresh cream.

The shift faded into early evening, the windows turning dusky blue and then black. I grated the ginger and made the icing glaze. I piped in the lemon-infused cream. Holding my hand a few inches above the tray, I dropped soft pinches of powdered coconut and watched them dust the tops of the puffs. Pretty, like snow. I thought about Lucia a few times. My performance was already becoming hazy in my memory: a few blurry moments—looking at myself in the bathroom mirror, the Stones song, wiping my trumpet with the tie, shaking her hand at the end, the high as I walked the streets home—and everything blurry in between. Each time, my blood quickened again, came alive with small sparks. Lucia was an imposing figure and I could still see her clearly, her parted hair tied back, her serious face that occasionally broke open in a smile; I remembered how that felt. I liked that Al guy too—he had a calm, unlaboured friendliness. Another Elijah or Ange maybe. Built for a long life in service to strangers. Everything rolling smoothly off his back.

A few people had ordered the fresh pastry, which pleased me; I knew it was best right now. I saw them going out on small saucers, watched them on Ange's and Elijah's trays. I felt happy. My little things going off into the world. Ending up with someone, being enjoyed. I was packing up and storing most of them in the freezer and cooler. Marc was in the cooler, checking out produce and taking notes. He came out and started pulling on his coat.

"Well, I'm off. I'll see you tomorrow, Peter. Hope you get that gig. Salottino's a nice place."

"Hey thanks, Marc."

"Maybe it's your big ticket."

There was no such thing. "Maybe," I said.

He left as Stu was coming to the back. His shift done, Stu was pulling off his apron and washing his hands. I would be helping Sadil through the first part of dinner—Sadil liked fewer shifts but long ones, often ten or twelve hours, so he would stay on grill for lunch and dinner. Sadil was a quiet, serious man, easy to work with. Once, after he heard I played an instrument, we talked about his father playing guitar. His mother had died and, grieving and alone, his father bought a cheap guitar and started playing every day. Perhaps it didn't help enough—his father died a few short years later. They had been in their eighties, Sadil explained. But I thought it was such a tender thing, a grieving widower picking up a guitar in the last years of his life. I wondered what songs he learned to play, whether he sang or not. I knew his old hands must have ached. Sadil hadn't said. It was my longest conversation with him; usually he kept to his work.

Stu was getting his coat on. "See you tomorrow? Unless you have a concert somewhere?"

"Yeah, see you tomorrow."

He smiled and zipped up. The joke caught me. The smile, and his relief earlier in the shift. I forgot sometimes that I was probably Stu's closest friend. That made me feel sad, in a couple of ways. "Bye, Stu," I said to his back as he was leaving. He turned his head slightly and tipped up his arm to show he had heard as he went out the back door.

I walked back to the schedule and checked who else was in tomorrow—Ange was off, Danielle was taking her shift and working until close. I was working in the evening too. I saw all the lottery tickets loosely stacked on the side of Marc's desk. I guess he hadn't won. I imagined the repetitive disappointment of that, what it took for him to keep going. And then I remembered my trumpet at home, the black case on the little table—repetitive disappointment, trying over and over—and I saw what it was. Small hope, in anything.

LATE OCTOBER

I DRIFTED the aisles from memory. I didn't browse anymore; I knew what I wanted and where it was, but now I walked slower, drifting.

This was the point of therapy, I guess—getting vaguely lost in familiar places while your past resurfaced like clouds, rising and obscuring the ordinary. This must be part of it, the reason they bounce you out before the hour is up. I usually went to the grocery store alone, no Christopher, no Sarah, on my way home from work. The grocery store terrorized my mother my whole childhood—there was too much stimuli, aisles and shelves and products and people. Lineups were hell. She would embarrass herself, people would see, she could never go back.

I admit it was colourful in there. Boxes and cans and sacks of loose things—rice and beans and noodles and corn. Humans were busy little creatures, obsessed with choice. We didn't have one of any thing, we had eight of every thing. Kidney beans. You'd think you would just buy a can without much thought, but there were three companies putting kidney beans in cans and fighting for your kidney bean dollars. And even the dried ones in bags—two kinds. What was the margin on beans? It must have been pennies, yet here we were, five brands total, me recalling which one I usually bought and trying to recall if I liked them. Someone wrote a book about how humans weren't supposed to have this much choice, that biologically it was unnatural, and I think they even talked about grocery stores—something about the exhaustion of choice. I didn't pick up the book but I remembered my first thought—what about people, how much human selection we had? We started brushing against thousands of people a day, and it was tiring—it made people lonely, they said. But I couldn't stay online for very long; I was too competitive or sarcastic or something to ever come close to enjoying it. It didn't make me think about myself, though, it made me think of my mother. That life of hiding.

A woman was walking down the aisle with an excessive number of children, some were visible but more were trailing behind her legs. I always got judgmental about that; I never knew why, it didn't affect me. But it always stuck out and became a string of stereotypes that drained me of enthusiasm for other people, for strangers. So many kids. After a while, she must have started ignoring them just to survive. And who's the father here? Just mindlessly breeding. But I saw those ignored kids forgotten at the end of the aisle and jogging to catch up; my senses were confused by the beauty of young children briefly alone, realizing it, seeing the world startling and anew, trotting off on light feet. I don't know what I resented from such a pretty wild thing.

Maybe the world needed more pretty wild things forgotten in crowded homes—maybe it was better than the nervous, over-attended solo children. Sensing their own importance, equating mistakes with death.

I was standing with the pasta now. Talk about choice—we were down to eating the exact same ingredient, but in different shapes. Just shapes.

Mom had been medicated in her later years, but it was too late. She had lived enough time in near total isolation that she forgot what reasons everyone else had for leaving the house, so she stayed home. Found a hole to die in. I had become crueller to her as the years progressed, almost testing myself, after years of care, seeing how far I could stretch in the other direction. She died last year, and honestly I did not stop to grieve—I moved it to the side and kept going. I did the funeral and moved on. Isabelle, wow, did she ever disapprove of that. She was short on words but her face contracted sharply when I said I didn't grieve. Curious, calculating, a mathematician registering an error. More than anything she could have said, it shamed me, that involuntarily tight pull of her face.

And of course. The detail that followed.

I met Mateo shortly after I was told my mother's cancer diagnosis. And I pursued him, consumed with both desire and fear—and when I heard her cancer was terminal, I pursued with something darker, something like hatred. And the hatred was not for my mother but for the space she took in my life—pain, only pain. The ceaseless pain, and the ultimate and final intimacy of someone else's death. That responsibility, I knew, would be mine.

In the next aisle stood a man by himself. He looked at me briefly and then a second time, a little longer. Our ages were probably within a couple years, and so a pause, consideration. Two animals sizing each other up. In my periphery I saw a muscular build and short stature with a clipped head that may have been a little small. I assumed his six to eight children were at home.

In the next aisle I was with the cereals—any sane person would have to agree there were too many cereals. Really, how many corn products did you need in various shapes and colours and flavours? They'd put a bird or cat character on the front to hook the kids and differentiate, but it was all corn, all glucose, all colouring. Corn or wheat, the entire market. Exhaustive and exhausting. Yet an immaculate machine. Resentfully I admired it, because I knew this garbage cost fractions of pennies, and every kid on the continent was hooked, every parent grudgingly participating in yet another segment that was fast, easy, and cheap. That was the direction we were going in, I guess.

Agoraphobia must have been some type of sensitivity, a misregistering and mislabelling of everyday experiences— things unnoticed by everyone else were an apocalypse of indignity to an agoraphobe. You were supposed to forget almost all of what you saw in every moment as a part of processing and survival—for the human animal, all animals— but of course once in a while, one animal simply could not ignore as much. Some were super-processors, they experienced everything and sometimes two levels too deep, and it was a terror on the sensory system—things would break down. And, vulnerable, they would hide.

Or at least that's how I saw it. I read a few articles on the many iterations of anxiety, and it seemed to me that some animals processed too much at once, ahead and behind, and sometimes they seized up in a life-stopping clutch.

That's how I thought about my mother, my grandfather—about Peter and me, better but still somehow bruised. All of us lined up. My mother tried to leave the house for minor errands but often failed; during one stretch she didn't leave our neighbourhood, our street, for almost six years.

What kind of life was that?

She was so high-strung I imagined it was plenty of stimulation for her to exist near windows and watch the occasional car driving by or someone walking a dog. But really. What kind of life? Maybe it was better a long time ago—maybe in a village, you only really knew about twenty people. Maybe you never left home, and in the fields and pastures you were always alone. Being alone with the work and the land and the unforgiving weather, sharing your world only with birds in distant trees.

I watched my mother's unused life slowly expiring over almost forty of the years I had been alive and I knew I would use mine, no matter the damage, no matter the flaws as people saw them—I knew that hollow judgment from up high, from tiny windows. I had been there too. But I would tell Isabelle, I would explain to her what I was doing. I was going to use my life.

I lingered in the produce section. It was a rich, moist forest of colours and textures. I looked around at the spread, slowly collecting bright hues and dark leaves.

And what about me?

I gave fifteen years to one company—rare for talent—and they snapped the reward from me. Now what. Just started my forties and I was supposed to be finding a cool, thin stream of recompense, some liquid gold reward, something that acknowledged everything I had done and paid for it. That was the VP job. That was supposed to be my compensation, and when it was removed so briskly and idiotically, I realized I had been working for years for free. And it wasn't about money, I made enough. I wanted the job, I wanted to be at the table. I wanted to own something. I resented people making mistakes and pretending it didn't matter. It belonged to me, but they had made a mistake, and I hated that, it disgusted me. Too many people were blind or uncaring, and that's where we got mistakes from. I was making a mistake with Mateo—and I continued making it—but it didn't fall into one of those categories: mine was intentional, almost vindictive, killing something about myself I didn't like anymore. Had relied on for so long, but no longer needed.

Mateo. What did I like about him, Isabelle had asked me. And the best I could find was that we had traits in common. A lusty aggression and deep resentment for the world, for one.

Some of the loose potatoes were sprouting little eyes. The produce staff didn't pull them promptly enough and they were forming new lives, there in plain view, all of us strangers seeing them in transition, in rebirth. Tender greens reaching out. Formerly potatoes, now little green shoots. What becomes of them, do they form leaves? Why aren't we eating potato greens? They must taste sour or give you loose stool or some other unpleasant thing.

They took that job from me and, smiling blandly, they continued with their daily lives—and expected me to continue as well. The thin, wan smiles of middle management who arrive after the success of people who sweat and try and care.

I looked around the produce section. Older men and women were testing fruits in their hands, turning over bunches, examining peppers.

What else did I like about Mateo? His entire body, for two.

I was talking to Isabelle now in my wandering moments

and explaining things to her. This must be a part of it too. I wanted Isabelle to understand and I never said it right in that room with eighteen minutes left. I stood in front of about seven linear feet of yellowing bunches of bananas, stacked heavily together. Bananas seemed to have only one brand. Actually, most fruit and vegetables. How could the margins be narrower than beans? The labours of farming—even just the size of those machines. The distances the food had to travel. Sarah loved bananas but Christopher did not. He ate them without enthusiasm, it was an action performed. I lingered over a smaller bunch; it was a tight cluster that seemed close to each other, like a family.

I thought briefly of Christopher eating a banana without enthusiasm and realized I had not described him much to Isabelle aside from basic sketches around his family, how we met, his work. And she had not asked much. I imagined she took cues from my early answers; maybe I hadn't been enthusiastic enough.

Christopher brushed just over six feet with his tight shoulders and forward-leaning neck. He was a bit stooped sometimes, at the end of the day. He was lean, his fair brown hair softening at the temples into an early forties grey. He was comfortable in his body, smooth-gaited, when he was alone. With others he sort of threw his head back a little, stood a little taller, and his limbs were pinched, stiffened somewhat by self-consciousness. I think he was a bit of a loner, but not an unhappy one. He fell into step with the herd easily enough, he blended in well, he was happy to do it. I liked that about him. I thought we shared it, although I saw myself as less happy.

Christopher had had a good childhood with good parents. For years I didn't trust it; in some dark corner I privately searched for his parents' flaws but, as clean and exquisite as new snow on Christmas morning, they loved each other. And they were good to their children without fail. Then, for some years, I thought they might be stupid; perhaps a dim intelligence took the heat from their arguments and the imagination to seek happiness elsewhere. But I was wrong there too. They were bright people with lively humour and simply had no wounds, no cruelty in them. For that reason, I thought, Christopher's forehead was smooth and his brow was clear. I never caught him staring off, lost in thought, with that look some people have. With heaviness. Christopher had one sister and one brother, everyone fair and lean, married and comfortable. I had met him more than ten years ago at a cycling event. Natalie from work had said: *Hey, Stasia, meet my friend Chris.*

We had built a sturdy thing of our marriage with fewer storms than I had expected from any union as a young woman. I thought marriage would be all fire and scars. He was patient and humorous and, seeing how good it was, I took his lead. Christopher wouldn't say anything funny for five or six days, then devastate you with some absurdity or self-deprecation that showed a kind of slow-burning appraisal of our odd little existence. The turtle thing. We had been eating breakfast and he was turning through the pages of a magazine when he stopped on a photograph of a politician and his family—they all look like turtles, he said. Then, turning through the rest of the pages, he lingered on almost every image—you know, everyone is kind of a turtle. And then I couldn't turn it off. Now, sitting in front of Isabelle one day a week, I could only see her as a turtle with a generous face and heavy jaw, the tilt of that round head over the compact body, the slightly angular glasses. I could draw her for a children's book: Isabelle the Therapy Turtle.

I was still around the bananas. I hadn't moved for a few moments, standing and staring at the chubby fists with their thick yellow-green fingers. Sometimes I struggled to reassign my brain from this new impulse to tell someone something, to describe, to tell, to tell, to tell. I picked up a bunch and put it in my cart, looking around. No one had taken any notice. Some people were lost in their own vegetation as well, poring a bit too long over the romaine, thoughts scattering like small, fallen stones.

I unloaded my groceries and watched the cashier's hands move each item over the scan. Her body was headless; I realized I had never looked up to see her face and, realizing the rudeness, I looked into her eyes and greeted her, smiling. Her lips pressed, mirroring, but relaxed again before becoming a smile. She did not make an impression on me; I did not make an impression on her. So we would pass as strangers, impressionless, a form of ignoring we all knew well, our survival in the churn of faces. I bagged my groceries and lifted them into the cart, then pushed them into the lot, then lifted them into the back of the car. The air was cool, the early evening going a bit blue; getting inside and closing the door and being done with it, but not home yet, spread out before me. Warm. I did this every week but it always felt like an accomplishment— astonishing how childhood patterns become the rhythm of life. I rummaged in my purse for a reward.

Fuck, I was going to smoke myself to death just sitting in the car. Not standing atop a cliff silhouetted against a late October sky, not walking through a whispering field of tall grasses, not alone behind a house in the dark where you hear fading trails of voices coming out the windows. All great places to smoke.

No, I was just sitting in a car in a parking lot—either at work, or a hotel, or the store. Up front and reclined in an upscale sedan smoking myself to a black-throated death. A corpse dusted with cigarette ash. My body rotting in the leather seats as the seasons passed, one by one. My lifeless skull tilted back on the headrest. My car towed to free up the parking spot again. My skeleton sitting in an impound lot, surrounded by rangy, pacing German shepherds, totalled cars, burned-out frames, rusted corpses, all of us waiting to be compressed, melted, and extracted. All of us waiting for one impossibly distant day, to be reborn.

* * *

My phone went off softly, sputtering and impatient. I sat up and silenced it, slid my legs out from under the covers and pushed them into cold slippers. Christopher needed a cold bedroom to sleep, so the slippers, the floor, were always unfriendly in the mornings. He was rolled onto his back with an arm over his head.

Downstairs was even colder. I had put on some heavier sweats and knee-high socks underneath, even though I knew they would slide down my legs about ten minutes in. I stretched, mostly the legs but the arms a little too. I zipped up my coat.

Outside was coldest, like a slap. It was still dark. I had my hood string drawn around my face and I turned south for a gentle downhill slope to warm up, feeling my legs loosen and soften like springs. I was alone on the streets, except for the cars and their wide, staring headlights. I turned off into small side streets, picking up a pace I would try to hold. A pace a bit above what I really wanted to do. Here, along a quiet stretch where all the bedroom windows were still dark, I lengthened into a sudden sprint and, forty seconds in, as pain tore at my sides, I fell back into my pace—it was now a relief.

My body was stirring and the cold air now worked with me, refreshing, and the good hormones came flooding down. The skies were nearing dawn, aching with blue, vaguely holy. But the soft high would burn out and pass over the next twenty minutes, and soon I would be working through pain and discomfort, and this, at last, was where I was cleanest and most honest with myself—I was best burning through pain. Yoga was too slow, sports too distracting, cycling too pleasurable when you could sit back and coast. When you ran, you were fully alone and present—muscles taut and tearing, fighting through it, fighting past it, rounding the next block, rounding the next one, until you were going in circles because turning felt so good, because you had to slow half a pace. Gratitude for the smallest things. When you could feel so big for such small things, you were on the way up. Buoyant.

Until, of course, it was too much. I broke. I stopped running and stood gasping, half-blind, resting my hands on my knees for a moment before reaching my arms up, hands clasped over my head, breathing and breathing.

Movement caught my eye. An old man came out of a house with an old dog on a leash. Both were hunched and moving slowly, carefully. The sun wasn't up yet; their silhouettes shuffled along the lamp-lit brick wall before they reached the driveway.

If only you pay attention, you are always shown how quickly it all ends in a tired, well-worn path.

I came into the house with my left ankle ragged, close to an hour later. Christopher was in the kitchen setting up the coffee maker. "Long run?" he asked without turning around. He was pushing buttons on the brewer.

"Yeah," I said. "A longer one."

"You have the thing this morning."

"Yeah, I know."

I went upstairs and Sarah was awake, sitting up in bed with damp hair and a dozen stuffed toys strewn across her blanket like lost little bodies, face up and face down. She didn't like choosing and wanted all of them in her bed with her. "Hey, Mom," she said absentmindedly, pushing toys aside to get to the edge of the mattress.

"You need a brush for school?" I asked.

"Yeah."

I sat down behind her with the brush, relaxing and readying. Mind slowly closing into a small, quiet thing. I ran the brush along the tips of her hair to detangle them. She sat upright and wasn't in a talkative mood, so she played with a horse instead. It had silvery hair and hooves, a horn too—actually, it was a unicorn.

"When's the last time I combed this for you?" She had been trying it herself some days.

"Tuesday."

"Ah, Tuesday," I said.

I ran the brush through the middle of her hair and down, repeating the motion in short strokes, down and down. Her hair gave off a lazy, golden fragrance.

Where it was more tangled near the top of her head, I carefully worked out the knots one at a time. My shirt was still damp from the run.

"When's the last time we cut this?"

"Summer," she said.

"Yeah, okay," I said. "But we didn't cut so much." I worked through a tough knot at the top of her head; she had to lean back for me to pull it apart with the comb. "It grows so fast," I said.

The soft combing eventually became smooth, the tangles fell apart, the hair now silken and easy. I kept running the brush through it in a slow, repetitive rhythm. The soft scent rising from her hair stirred something in me again, not like the running, but a body awareness that absented my mind—a physical thing that eclipses all other things, darkens them. I had a collection of these things. It was curious, I had ways of passing time without my thoughts trailing along and flattening everything. The brush caught little snaps of electricity from her hair, and spare threads rose, floating. I kept brushing with a fluid, steady pull, drawing something out. Sarah was quiet for a while.

"Mom, are you done?"

I remembered the dampness of my hair against the back of my neck, my shirt.

I put the brush down without saying anything.

I let Christopher get Sarah ready for school and drop her off. I stood under the shower, facing away, letting the hot water run over my shoulders and down the front of my body, my head hanging limp between my shoulders, collecting myself.

The neighbour down the street, Vanessa, her daughter died the week before. Eighteen years old, just off to college, crossing an intersection on campus, hit by a pickup—gone. Everything over. Vanessa was a single mother and this was her only child. Eighteen years, over.

I slipped into a black dress and put on black eyeliner, nothing else. I would stop at the florist on the way to the visitation. I told Christopher not to miss work and I didn't want Sarah there—I was sparing both of us: Sarah from the death, me from shielding her from the death. Plus she had school. But she would take any opportunity to miss school.

The florist was impressed with my order. She smiled shyly, binding the flowers with cream ribbon, not knowing where I was going. I laid the three dozen Vendela roses carefully into the back seat and checked the address on my phone before getting in the front. I felt them behind me, all three dozen, as if alive.

The funeral home was a brown brick building with white pillars at the front. Pulling into the lot, I saw mostly smaller, cheaper cars parked into tidy rows; I circled and found an empty section at the back. It was interesting how money moved together—people with money spent their time with other people with money. At wedding and funeral parking lots, there'd be almost all nice cars or all ordinary cars—little flocks. If I died, honestly, at this point, it would be mostly nice cars at my funeral. I killed the engine and sat there thinking about a cigarette. Was it a weird detail to notice, about the cars? I may have been distracting myself. I was here because of a dead girl.

I decided against the cigarette and got out of the car, holding the roses in my arms. They were luxurious; they were not a serious or mournful flower, but indulgent and opulent. A distraction. But they were so childlike in that way, achingly beautiful. And three dozen, cradling them, they were almost warm and breathing, some kind of living offering. I didn't know how else to do this.

The room was long and low, wood-panelled and lit with small glass lamps. The carpet was a dusty deep red and there were some pieces of modest wooden furniture around, chairs and benches and cabinets. The room was warm and half filled with people—the casket was at the far end, dark red. I looked at it again: the colour was blood. So that was the girl, Rita, who had curly black hair and slightly crooked front teeth that had made her look mischievous as a young girl—and later, as she got older, made her look knowing. Closed casket, she had been crushed under the truck. And just like that, over.

I knew immediately where Vanessa was standing but could not look at her.

I went to the casket instead, walking the length of the room without looking at the others. I laid the roses close to the end of the coffin, at the girl's feet—they were so heavy and plush they started to slide off the casket and I pulled them back, but overcorrected; now they slid toward the front. I adjusted them back and forth until they rested, balanced, on the curve of the red wood. I tried to be discreet as a few heads turned. It pulled me out of the moment—was it funny or awful? Maybe neither. But the roses were gorgeous on the wood, heartbreaking at her feet. The large photograph of Rita was not a good one; posed with a professional background, it didn't show the real girl, not the experience of her alive. Smaller photos around the room caught that wild smile and chaotic hair, a laughing girl approaching womanhood, clumsy and confident, full cheeks flushed. Young women, there was something about them—incandescent, especially when shy.

Without the roses in my arms, I was naked standing there. I couldn't look at Vanessa. I couldn't know how it felt, seeing it in her face. I couldn't meet her eyes, mother to mother. I knew enough types of grief to know I had never come near the big one, the wide void that would claim the rest of her life. I rummaged through my bag but didn't know what to pull out; it couldn't be a phone, so I let the bag fall to my side again. I couldn't do this.

I felt weak. I remembered my longer run in the morning; I hadn't eaten after. Or it was nerves. I walked to the edge of the room and sat on a bench, looking around but not seeing the people, instead seeing pant legs, pantyhose legs, and black shoes. I didn't feel like crying either. I did not know what my presence here meant. I didn't know why, for any of this. The room moved softly to the left, then to the right; I recognized the climbing hum of adrenaline as my body knew very well what I was trying to face. But I could not look at Vanessa. Could not meet her eyes. Her grief would move into my body, and there was not enough in me, nothing that immense.

There was a box and notepaper and envelopes on a cabinet. Seeing it suddenly changed me, relief washed down— I had a purpose, an action. I got up from the bench and walked over, I picked up a piece of notepaper and a pen, and considered writing something. But I was standing there in front of everyone, the room growing silent and thick around me, overwhelming. I put the paper and pen down and picked up an envelope instead. My back to the room, I unclipped my bracelet and slipped it into the envelope. Just as it fell heavily, safely, into the bottom, I brought the envelope up to my lips to moisten and seal it. I put it in the box. It hit the bottom with a thick sound.

I left the visitation. A group of people surrounded Vanessa and I passed them, going outside, lighting a cigarette as I walked to the back of the lot where my car was—my nicer, expensive car. I got inside and, very easily, like a second wash of relief, started crying. It didn't make a sound, it wasn't real crying, just tears rolling slowly down my cheeks as I started the car and, after circling the empty back row, left the lot.

* * *

"You seem far away."

"Oh, sorry—" I sat up and adjusted a pillow. "—I just fell this way." I lay down with my head brushing the edge of his shoulder, my hair falling down his arm.

"No, I meant in your head."

In your head. His odd phrasing, sometimes; he'd spoken a mix of Italian and English growing up. I was tempted to smile but it didn't seem right for how he had said it, a little cautiously. He was not particularly cautious by nature. "Oh, right. Distant." I was looking up at the ceiling. "It's the therapy. My mind wanders... Sometimes I keep going with the session after I leave, talking to her, or to myself, explaining things, describing things."

He looked at the ceiling too, and didn't say anything.

Mateo was described amply to Isabelle because she had asked for it, sniffing around. Poor woman, I thought. Listening to everyone's illicit affairs with her wall of certificates and going home to her monogamous partner and respectful children, having a nutrient-dense meal with one glass of wine, and sleeping soundly for eight straight— detached in almost every way. Attachment meant contact, sometimes striking, sometimes blows. For me, anyway. I'm sure she had troubles; they were addressed and communicated and resolved before they became interesting. I told her about Mateo, his heavily lidded eyes in that wide, flat face, full lips that separated easily, flashing teeth, his ancient Roman nose and black brows—actually I didn't say any of these things, but I thought them as I told her about his alcoholic father, abandoned and vindictive mother, four younger sisters—yes, four—and the three dogs he grew up with in the country. They were poor. The animals got scraps and scavenged on nearby properties; they were the sad, darting shadows of his childhood, spines and rib cages showing. He had showed me a photo. He loved dogs of course, and had two now.

He didn't talk so much but patiently explained when I had asked, giving a few details, and I imagined the rest. And those details were the lock. The irregular pieces of him fit into the irregular pieces of me, clicking together—it wouldn't work if we were both smooth and whole. Another cliché. That's what Isabelle and I were doing, counting clichés.

Mateo was intelligent but his body did not look that way. He was stout and muscular, like a refrigerator; he looked built for labour, lifting things or dragging them or pushing them down hills. He did not educate himself with ideas or abstract things: he was a millwright. But his mind was nimble and aggressive, his opening shot mocking, he did not welcome strangers into his life, preferring to establish his solitude before anybody thought they might try to know him. *Hello and fuck you*, he said to everyone with bored eyes. And yet, somehow, almost friendly with it, a bearishly oversized pup cuffing you down with a paw—serious but never mean. Still, so bruised and arrogant, a true unknowable. He did not like kissing; he used his mouth but did not kiss. He was so proud, he could not even lower himself to marry—it was an obscenity to be owned that way.

He was hired as part of a consultant team to help us build and operate the machines that cut the leather trim and fitted the brass detailing on our bags. He was in the factory for two months, a project I managed directly. I remember how his face changed when we met, vacant and bored but polished professional, suddenly sharpening as I came over. It was my project and I was on a warpath, utterly humourless in every way. I remember how his face came alive, how the eyes focused as if waking. At the end of the project, we had moved quickly.

"So are you cured yet? The therapy."

"What do you mean—cured of what?" I asked, rolling my face to the side, looking at him, his profile still tipped toward the ceiling.

"Whatever problem you're going for."

"No, it's not like that."

I remembered that profile, its first impact. He had been showing me something and I looked at his brow and nose and lips silhouetted against the pale table stretched below him—"Do you understand?" he had asked, and "Yes, of course," I had said—but I had heard not a word of it and later had to email to ask for a written explanation. "You weren't listening, I could tell," his patient admonishment came back. And he explained everything again, carefully. I felt it was somehow intimate. I had felt everything was intimate. When you feel intimate with a stranger, you're gone—you've been pulled away from your life. Everything that had been close with you was now strange, everything distant was now close, and you were not going to be able to turn it back.

"I thought maybe this was bothering you." His voice was flat.

"It's about work," I said. "I went because I didn't get the promotion. I snapped—something in me." I waited a few moments for him to understand. "And I guess some of it goes back to my mother." Now there was something in my chest: I didn't want to burden him with this, I wanted to be alone with it. But he was asking something and I was trying to make him understand. Something yawned open on the bed, a wide vulnerable thing.

"You never talk about her," he said.

"She died last year," I said.

He turned his face to me, then started to sit up with his arm underneath him. "You didn't tell me that."

I spoke carefully. "That's not what this is about."

I looked up at the ceiling and waited. He lay back down on the bed and was still for a while, hands resting on his ribs, gently rising with his breath, the corner of my eye on the movement.

Sarah strayed into my mind, her bright face and the quick movements across it, like light on water, her endless imagination, everything she created. Eyes like Christopher's. She picked her coloured hair elastics each morning and pored over the barrettes, choosing, her precision ambitious and hopeful about the day ahead. These will be perfect, today will be perfect.

Mateo moved again. "Okay," he said. He sat up and slowly brushed his hand along my arm, deliberate, with attention. It was smoothly done, a gesture performed, no instinct behind it. No contact. I let it finish its path. "You've been smoking," he said.

I started to sit up as well. "You can smell it," I said.

"A little," he said. Then, after a pause, "Okay," again. I saw his teeth briefly flash before his mouth closed tightly. He got out of the bed and started to collect his clothes, hanging on the edge of the bed, pulling his pants over his legs. His back was blacked out from the light in the bathroom. He pulled his shirt over. Something bothered him—the therapy, or my mother—it was rare for him to dress so soon. Maybe too personal, and retreating now.

But he was right, wasn't he? It's what Isabella saw first. That old intelligence of his waking up and seeing the ground change. What we were doing was either completely logical or completely illogical, and I couldn't get a grip on it; it spun wildly out of my hands in sharp twists. Talking about it made it worse, somehow it got farther away.

And there was always fear. Somewhere outside of the room, stalking the edges of the drive home, standing on street corners and looking at me, lifting each morning with the pale sun but again crowding the dark windows at night. The fear it was not going to be enough. This wasn't enough and we were still lonesome for something. And we couldn't find it, name it, know it. We were too much the same; we were going to smash each other and run. We were going to blame each other.

"Maybe the therapy will cure us both," I said lightly. I was hoping it would become softer and, like air, rise up and disappear. Become less true.

He didn't respond to that. I couldn't see his profile or whether his face changed. He finished dressing.

Alone, I pulled the covers around me, rustling, enjoying the crisp tuck under my legs. I felt it should be snowing. There was that feeling of it. After he'd left, I had opened the curtains but there was no snow. There was just a parking lot with a few cars and bare trees on the flat, scrubby grass. It was too early for it, only October, and I'm not sure why I felt that way. But it should have snowed.

WEDNESDAY

HEAD TO TOE, black. Nothing fancy about it—black pants, black button-up shirt, and my nicer shoes. I didn't go to be noticed or seen, just to be a dark figure in a dark room, one of many.

We closed at 10 p.m., and Hassan, Danielle, and I cleaned up and shut down for about half an hour. I had been wearing a knee-length apron, so my pants survived the shift. I changed my shirt in the bathroom and checked my wallet for the second time to see the white baggie, and I counted my twenties. My shoes had an unknown spattering on them, so I wiped them with a bit of paper towel I had wadded up and put under the tap for half a second. That was not a noticeable detail for anyone else, I did it for me.

It was cold outside, the coldest it had been this week. I liked it. It sent a bright shock down my throat and into my lungs, and the lights of cars and shops seemed sharper, fractured.

Hassan locked the door and the three of us said goodnight. White clouds of breath hung in the air around us as we turned and walked in separate directions—me crossing the street, south, Danielle going north to the subway, Hassan walking west, bare hands pushed down into his pockets.

Most Wednesday nights I did the same thing: I worked the closing shift, then I went downtown to a club we called Fifteen. Its real name was Veni, Vidi, Vici, marked outside with the letters VVV. But adding up the numerals, we called it Fifteen—VVV was awkward to say, and the full name even worse. You could tell if someone was new to the club when they said the letters or name, but when someone said Fifteen, you knew they knew—a secret handshake for the regulars.

Wednesday was an off-night, and it wasn't a high-end, expensive club. It had a bit of character, it was a bit crooked. But it had a great house DJ and the bartenders didn't care who you were—they got you drinks, fast. Even if you looked painfully ordinary. Those of us who went regularly grew quite fond of it, and anywhere else we went always felt cold and shallow. There was no lineup on a Wednesday night, no cover.

I walked south for a long time, then turned left. I passed a handful of clubs and their throbbing sidewalks outside. One place, Silk, usually had a lineup, even on an off-night—I walked by two women standing outside wearing furs. And a guy too, near the end of the line, there was actually a guy waiting in a fat fur coat. Those shaggy shoulders—ridiculous. But I was fascinated and pretended not to look closely as I passed, still catching the winks of light from huge diamond studs in his ears. I had my hat pulled low over my eyes; I wasn't the kind of guy he would notice.

I crossed the intersection just before Fifteen and again remembered the convertible. I had even started calling it Convertible Corner to myself, this intersection, waiting at the light. It was a scene I couldn't seem to describe properly to anyone—although I tried, a lot, usually while drinking. And yet I couldn't shake the image either.

This past summer I had been coming here on a Wednesday night, a balmy July dusk, one of those midsummer dusks that fades slow. The sun had set hours before but the city cement was still warm. The air—the vertical stripes of sky still visible between the buildings—was glowing electric blue. And I was coming here, crossing this corner, and sitting at the red light was a white convertible, top down, full with five people. Two guys in the front, three girls in the back. The girls had sat up on the backs of the seats, so they were higher than anyone else. Everyone was young and everyone was beautiful. But they were stopped at the light for a couple of minutes, so the guys turned the music down and, in the awkward pause on the corner—all of us watching them—in that moment, everyone in the car got out their phones. I stared at it all, witnessing something; I don't know what. Crossing in front of the car, I looked directly into the open convertible facing me. Music down. Everyone on phones.

I kept trying to describe this scene to people. Sometimes even strangers, when I had been drinking. The image, the picture of it in my mind, had stuck somewhere; I guess it was so funny and lonely, both. I think everyone assumed it was something about phones, some condemnation, a tired complaint, but I don't know—that didn't feel like what I meant. Not all of it, anyway. It was something about those moments in life when we were most hopeful, the mundanely exotic things we wanted, the big nights in hot cars, the simple smallness of it all. The moments we were awkward and hopeful—with something innocent in that awkwardness. And that's the part that lingered, the only reason I remembered the white convertible. So in my mind it was Convertible Corner, this intersection, because I thought of it every time I crossed the street before I got to Fifteen. And I always looked up and down the streets as if I might see the car again, and I thought of them as I went down into the club—forgettably young and beautiful, forever innocent and awkward. Everyone longing for that Big Summer Night and all its memories, fading like a comet tail.

I got to Fifteen, with the big guy Cody standing outside in a black parka, no hat on his shaved head. The sidewalk pulsed slowly, thoughtfully. There was no lineup, so we just nodded at each other as I went in, tapping lightly down the steps into the basement. Cody didn't need to chat.

Here was the moment for sensory sensitivity—you could walk down into a place and feel your whole body change, like a lizard rippling in colour and heat. Fifteen was hot and dark, painted orange and black and gold. And the music, the bass—the earth pulled out from under you and then pushed back into your body. It was world-destroying and utter creation, almost religious. My life of twenty minutes ago was gone. This reality was a deep movement beneath that, unreal, exquisitely rendered.

But it was also just a club in a basement. I ordered a double rye and soda at the glowing bar. I drank it quickly, leaning back against the bar, looking at the sparse open area where people would start dancing in an hour or two. I waited for the next moment when the rye would spread a warm pool inside me. It did, unfailing. I ordered another double and moved off to the side to drink it slower.

Around the edges of the room was a raised platform with gold-topped tables, a few still empty. I sat at one. At the other tables sat couples, groups of friends, and a few other singles like me. We were waiting to get drunk or for a pill to kick in. Watching pots, waiting for them to boil. And then the DJ did something brilliant—she put on Wardyn.

A beat and bass line receded and slowly his sample— brooding and patient—crept in; I knew it immediately. I drained my drink until the ice clattered against my lips and I quickly got another, my legs warm and fluid now, my head hot and buzzed. I went back to my empty table. Next to me, a table of young men watched, wondering who I was. I didn't exactly look like one of those other creeps alone at the club—they were confused, young, tourists maybe; there in a small pack, searching hopefully for a similar pack of women. They didn't know what mid-thirties felt like, not on a Wednesday night, not after working in a kitchen. But they would one day. I felt benevolent, generous after the doubles; I raised my drink and gave them a small, warm smile. Embarrassed, they looked away.

The Wardyn sample moved along the edges of the room, woven with his chopped-up voice. The warmth in me formed a pulse, matching his. I knew Wardyn, downloaded him, read about him. A moody Irish guy, songwriter and DJ, absolutely brilliant, tall, lean, and pale, like a young tree in December. He looked like the loner at a party, the one everyone was nervous to approach—so distant and cool-faced. Maybe some kind of hero, an idea, for me. And he was handsome, legitimately handsome—classically, like a Roman in marble. Yet he wasn't famous, had just a few thousand followers online, and did short tours to small venues. I wonder how he handled that. He must have known he was brilliant, saw handsomeness in every mirror; I wondered if he wondered why he hadn't broken out yet. If he doubted himself. I didn't doubt him, but I did not trust the world to know either.

His sample shifted out sideways, the DJ slipping something else in. His broken voice echoed in falling notes, leaving me behind like an emptying room. I knew the reasons. I knew there were too many artists now, and fame was not rightful or owed. You could die unknown being *only* brilliant and handsome. The world was crowded now and no one knew who mattered or why. It was loud, and loudness seemed to win. Now you had to be clever and showy online, painfully casual, precisely natural. Even when it was real, it wasn't. From what I saw of Wardyn's shadowed brow and aloofness, I knew he would never break out. He wouldn't do cute videos. He would remain relatively unknown, having been brilliant only. I don't even know if he mourned that, or if I did alone—or if it was right.

I went to the bathroom for a bump.

A few guys were waiting for the urinal and a couple of us went into stalls. I used my hand, businesslike—smeared my gums, enjoying. I didn't like to touch anything else in a stall. I came out and washed my hands, looking in the mirror. I enjoyed the mirror now, which was rare for me. I straightened up, set my jaw, and allowed my eyes to meet themselves in the glass, and see everything behind me— the glittering details of the room. Red walls, black counters, glossy silver hand dryers, guys walking by, looking around and not looking around. Tall and skinny guys, big and muscular guys, short and wiry guys, medium-height and soft guys, everybody everywhere in between. Everyone in here was perfect, I felt. And I was among them. My heart was beating hard now, sure of itself, believing.

I came out of the bathroom, feeling large. I was halfway to drunk and an early high lifted my feet a few inches from the ground; I breathed through glowing lungs. I went to the bar and waited to order another drink. People were dancing now and I watched them, every individual circle of movement and the small, singular soul at the centre of it. If you could dance well, I admired you from a distance, the part of you that had no words. If you danced poorly, I loved you differently, as family, tender and close. As I imagined families were for some people. And then I saw Alex.

Alex was petite, high-pitched, and showed up often on Wednesday nights. We had had some interesting conversations once we started recognizing each other and knew we wouldn't ever be daytime friends—everything unnecessary was quickly shed. Alex tried being womanly but could not escape the genetic reality that she had absolutely no chin and quite puffy cheeks, looking slightly like a pugnacious child. Never looking older than about fourteen, and it didn't help that she was short. Still she wore a lot of makeup, fake lashes, trying to dress as she imagined an adult woman would—but always an odd caricature, somehow. Alex was somewhere in her thirties and an administrative assistant at a law firm who worked from home on Thursdays, and so, most Wednesday nights, she came out and got wrecked. We were friends in that. But she was also family in a way—she looked like a little kid dressed as a woman, and I knew that body betrayal. All my life I wanted to look impressive, interesting in almost any way—I knew how much that meant when you got up on stage and faced the room and pulled the instrument to your mouth. But I never did. I looked like a guy in a kitchen. I knew that weight for a long time.

A sample kicked up, a vocal—*watchin' others drink too much, much too soon*—I left the bar and strode over to Alex, moving smoothly through the crowd.

"Peter!" she cried out, clapping her hands together.

—*you found a life in the night*—

"Alex!" I said.

We hugged and pulled apart, nodding enthusiastically. She was with a woman I hadn't met, Candace. Candace was tall and strong-limbed, with aloof, wide-set eyes. Her yellow hair was pulled back and ran long down her spine.

"Hello, Candace!" I shouted.

"What's up, man?" she half shouted back. It seemed old-fashioned, the way she said it—laid-back nineties. She talked as if she could roll a joint thick as your arm.

"They should call this place Ten," I said.

"What?"

"Ten—they should call this place Ten."

Alex was looking back and forth between us.

Candace started laughing. "I don't get what you're saying, man."

"I only like the first two Vs," I shouted.

"Peter is a good friend," Alex said to Candace, by way of explanation. Then she laughed, high-pitched. "He gets drunk and talks nonsense!"

"Just Wednesdays," I told them. "On Tuesdays I make pastry puffs."

"Peter also plays the trumpet," Alex said.

We were shouting all this to each other over the music.

"Cool, man," Candace said, impressed now. She was attaching "man" to everything—for my benefit? It was unclear. "You make music?"

"No, I don't write," I said. "There so much out there already; I don't have anything to add. I just play sometimes."

"Right on." Candace turned to Alex. "I'm going to the bathroom. You good?"

"Yeah, I'm good," Alex said.

I looked around and realized we were about a third of the way onto the dance floor, with clusters of people all around us. "Are we dancing or are we getting a drink?" I asked.

"Drink! Drink! Drink!" Alex raised her arms and marched through the crowd.

We waited at the bar. "So, this Candace," I said. "Date? Friend? Drug buddy? Dance buddy?"

"Actually, I have no idea," she said in her small, laughing voice. "But whatever it is, it's temporary. She's visiting from out west, for a week."

"Oh, interesting," I said. "I'm not going to hover, okay."

"Okay," she said. "Thanks, Peter."

"You're buying, though?"

Alex spat out a laugh. "You shithead. Yeah—yeah I guess I'm buying."

"Poor musician, you know?"

We both were grinning. We were still waiting; a few people were ahead of us at the bar. The track rotated out and something slow was entering; I saw a dim outline of the DJ way at the back of the room standing in a yellow glow. The track had a loping rhythm, a gentle repeat, that pulled back the entire room—and everyone just sort of dropped into it. Watching a crowd surge and swell, then fall into a soft collapse, was a beauty to me. Everyone together—strangers, small flocks of friends.

Alex ordered me another rye and soda. We moved off, entering the crowd. So long, sobriety. Goodbye, faces—hello, outlines. Silhouettes etched in light. A hundred eclipses around me. I saw a lot of beauty when I was a bit lost, ripped, torn, thrown from the cliff. Surrounded by sightless strangers, riding an immaculate overlap of sedative and stimulant. Thrown from the cliff and into a warm, moving body of water.

Candace came and found us, her face smug. She felt good. All of us felt good.

"Candace, it was great to meet you," I said, offering my hand.

"Oh, cool," she said, surprised.

"I'm going to disappear in the crowd now."

"Oh, okay, man. Good to meet you too."

I left them. I drained the drink Alex had bought me, then faced the crowd, moving to the music. I went to the bathroom and came out again. Suddenly I got really comfortable. I was going fast but keeping up. I moved into the crowd, arms in the air, loose-limbed but shuffling like an old man, and found a dark space in the middle surrounded by people, none of them looking at me, and I rotated there, slow as a planet, feeling large and calm. The floor heaved up and down in a heartbeat, primal; colours and lights spun. I had my face up, then down.

I'd been doing this for long enough, I made rules for it—what the drinking and drugs would be for me. One day a week and no more. You can't be sad when you go. You'll end up always wanting it when you're sad. You can't have trauma; it was dangerous. You had to face that first, sober. You can't go when you're poor. You'll start cutting back on food, then bills, then everything slips. You can't be rich either. Rich people had a different sadness; they would slip too, and they could easily afford it. You can't fall in love with the drugs themselves: powders, pills, alcohol. You had to see them as doors and windows. Nobody loves the door or the window, you love what you see on the other side. And, above all, you couldn't wait for it all week, you had to love the other days first. The boring Tuesdays, the short and sad Sunday nights. All of life is Tuesdays and Sundays. You had to be bored and alone, and not do it, and go to bed with a quiet mind. You could never forget it's a little bit cheap, a little bit fake. Even though it's not cheap to you. But it is. You got better highs of terror and relief from performing for a stranger. From losing a trumpet and finding it again. From a stranger's random ask for kindness that broke open a world you thought you inhabited alone. I made rules for the drugs and kept them an arm's length away. I kept a cool relationship with pleasure, never fully trusting it; I would enjoy but not love, visit but not stay. But I loved the people, the weird-mouthed, strange-limbed dancers in the shimmering lights around me. I wanted to ask everyone, *Hey do you love this?* I wanted to hear, *Yes I love this*.

The DJ broke the floor. She held a sudden, devastating silence in the room—all of us paused. And held. And then she dropped it.

Small, broken variants of *hooooooo* leapt up from the crowd. How she pulled us apart, how she brought us all together—how a break and a drop made us into one. And the music, I loved the music. Songs that never ended, only turned into other songs. A woman near me was spinning, steady in her circle. She slowed and saw me, smiled. A vocal was drawn out around us *—and my brain's bruised from all of the bad news—and my brain's bruised*.

She stopped spinning and laughed suddenly. I didn't see her friends or who she was with. "Who are you?" she shouted.

"I make puffs! Pastry puffs!"

"Wow!"

"Only on Tuesdays." She should know the truth.

"Yeah!" she said.

We were messed up in a basement with loud music. The world was so big now, crowded.

"Who are you?" I shouted back.

"I write emails!" she shouted. "A lot of fucking emails!"

Crowded, and online so much worse. Too many people, everywhere, always. It pushed you smaller.

"I love emails!" I said.

"Not if you write them all day!"

A circle that went around. Brutally alone. Predictable and heartbreaking and as sudden as a snapped limb.

"Depends on the email, right?"

"Yeah." She nodded hard, fully into this point. "It depends on the email!" She laughed.

But here it was dark, and small.

I turned to give her space back and shuffled out of the crowd, toward the bar. Halfway there, I changed my mind and turned for the smoking patio out back; generous joints circled indiscriminately, and I wanted something deeper.

I stepped out onto the patio. The November night was brittle cold and the stars hung delicately in the blue-black sky. We knew the best drugs already. Wanted children, lives of humility and connection—we longed for other people, but only if they were kind to us. To each other. I stood next to some guys in light shirts, shivering. We nodded at each other as I stood close. Misanthropes were not born but cruelly made. Shy ones the same. The guy to my left leaned over with a reed-slim joint and I nodded, taking it and drawing a small, neat line of smoke between my lips. I handed it back quickly and looked the man full in the eyes. His face was almond-shaped and his black eyes seemed like the oldest thing I'd seen in my life. But he was young. "Thank you," I said.

Like something kicking through my chest, he smiled at me, ancient eyes unchanged. He brought the joint to his mouth again, his lips forming a tight circle for half a moment, and then passed it behind him to his friend. "No problem," he said.

I went back inside. Now this party was starting. Really fucking starting. I was in the Holy Trinity now; I would be chasing it, close to losing it all night. I would fall into the crowd and disappear. Surface occasionally, floating on my back, understanding.

"Peter!"

I snapped back into place.

"Peter!"

I turned around, saw a man beckoning—Billy. Of course, old Billy. He was in line at the bar, waving eagerly, childlike, with both hands. Billy was in his late fifties, thick-bodied, with a shaggy face and happy-dog eyes. He partied a lot. He came to Fifteen a lot, mostly on off-nights—I don't think he went much on weekends, a more serious crowd then. Billy was a well-dressed hippie who had started on uppers later in life, learning to dance through the night after he had dealt with all the obligations of marriage and family and career. I didn't know if he worked anywhere now, what his current situation was. I loved Billy because he said the strangest things, he made them feel normal.

I put my hands up in surrender. I approached him at the bar. He put his arms up in greeting, like hugs high above our heads. Stoned—either everything happened very slowly or it was over already and I don't remember how I got there. We were facing each other.

"Peter! When's the last time I saw you? Last Wednesday? Was it last Wednesday?" He was shouting. "Or the week before."

"Yeah, I was here last week, Billy."

"Did I buy you a drink?"

"Yeah, you did."

"Let's do that again."

Billy faced the bar and tried to lean past another person ahead. His shouts were lost in the music. Billy wore all black too; he liked to disappear and not be seen, like me. I know he felt we were the same, in this and other ways. On the outside he was a hippie in hair only—longish, wavy, silver; it moved softly around his face and when nightclub lights caught it, it flamed out, neon, wild. The rest of him was crisp.

He handed me the rye. "How was that audition?"

"I told you about that?"

"Yeah, you told me about that. Pretty shit drunk last time I saw you. Nervous and all that. I bet you were fine."

"I was pretty good, Billy."

"So when do you know?"

"When do I know what?"

"When do you know if you got it or not?"

"Oh, Thursday, she said," I said. "Tomorrow I guess."

"Thursday tomorrow?"

"Yeah."

Billy took a drink and passed his eyes across the room. "I know you are the right one, but they are allowed to be wrong," he said.

I didn't say anything.

"I mean, if you don't get it, it's okay."

I saw it. He was trying to let me down gently.

"I know that, Billy. It's just a temporary gig anyway. Not a life-changer."

"Hey, we don't always know what life-changers are until they change our lives. You can't predict that." Billy was becoming wise. Hippie wisdoms came out of him like Pez. We were still half shouting, standing beside each other.

"Billy, I can't tell which way you're going."

"What?"

"Are you trying to comfort me in advance by saying I might not get it?" I paused because the music had built up before crashing again. "I might not get it, but then you're saying it might have been a life-changer?"

Billy pressed his lips together and nodded, taking a drink. "Yeah, OK, mixed messaging there, Peter. But I meant what I said."

"Which part?"

"All of it."

I drank. "Billy, I had a buzz going and now I'm thinking about that audition."

He dodged it. "Anything beautiful lately?"

I knew what he meant. It was an ongoing conversation with us. "Yeah. Coming home from the audition."

"Well." He gestured with his open hand.

He meant the few tiny moments that were exquisite and immaculate, natural and fleeting—and rushes of that feeling, almost blushing. So earnest, I felt many times Billy was a child himself, innocent and excited, eager to share.

"Coming home, I felt like everything was right. Like I was on fire."

"High," Billy said, nodding.

"Yeah. It was kind of perfect."

We didn't say anything for a moment.

"My neighbourhood felt different. I felt different walking home, people around me were more real. There was so much leftover adrenaline in me, felt like I could run for hours. Sprints. Over tops of cars."

"Flying."

"Yeah."

"That's perfect," he said. "Being alive like that." He grinned. "I take pills for that."

I saw Alex and Candace laughing and heading to the bar. They looked happy. Seeing that made me happy, mirror that I always was. I thought about Lucia and Al. I thought about Marc sitting at a messy desk and Stu pausing a video game to take a swig from a green bottle of pop. I thought of Ange sitting on a balcony listening to music. I didn't know much about these people. Some of them I saw almost every day. I'm not sure why it struck me then, drunk and stoned in a basement club with Billy, that I didn't really know them. Billy and I were facing the crowd of dancers.

"I tell you about the yellow chair yet?" He smiled at me from the side.

"No." But it felt familiar—it felt forgotten already, as if I had been too high to remember. But I didn't want to tell him that.

"Oh, good. I was waiting, I guess." He considered that, then continued. "The yellow chair. Well, I drive up this same road all the time—I go in the mornings, it's an errand I like to get out of the way. And I go up this road and there are these big fields on either side where the electrical lines are. You know—those towers that have the wires—I forget now."

"Hydro lines."

"Hydro lines—transmission lines. Yeah. It's a big empty industrial field with tall grasses, weeds, no sidewalks or paths in there. Rough land. And I see a yellow chair in there. Sitting in there, by itself. Like a metal chair painted yellow." Billy took a drink. "At first I think it's just a chair somebody forgot in the field but I'm driving through often enough that I start to notice—I see the chair in different places each time." He started gesturing with his free hand, the other still holding a drink. "Every couple of weeks, couple feet this way. Another time, turned a little bit, facing a different way. Just slightly. So I'm thinking, somebody's sitting in that chair."

The yellow chair. I remembered now. *Somebody's sitting in that chair*. I remembered him describing it.

"Then last Friday, I couldn't get to the store in the morning. I have to go later. And now I'm driving on that road and it's four or five in the afternoon and the sun's going down. November sunset. Like somebody tore the sky open and on the other side was fire. More than that—green around the gold, blue around the green. Devastating. You know that chair is facing west. So I'm understanding it now.

"There's some housing around there—row houses. Standing alone next to some empty lots, before the empty fields. And there's a long-term storage company—rows of metal garages, a driveway, a small office at the gate. Nothing else."

He had been loosely gesturing how the pieces were placed together but he stopped talking. The club was crowded and waves of people moved with the music, rippling around the room, and the whispery high from the joint made everything seem slow. I wondered how long we had been standing there. A couple of dancers had their hands in the air as if skimming the sound with the tips of their fingers. Lights winked on and off, illuminating one person, casting another in shadow, before rotating again;

Billy was facing them but he was miles away, inside his own little world, letting me in—he was so happy and so lonely, both.

"It's not really about the yellow chair, of course—but what an elegant image, anyway—now I just think about that person. That person in the chair." Billy put one finger up, let his hand drop again. "I think about the front-desk person at the storage facility. Or a security guard. Someone in those row houses. I think it has to be someone nearby. And I like that they go there. I like that they sit in that metal chair even in November and watch the sun go down. I like that they move it sometimes. Maybe they have a cigarette, or a joint. But I like that nobody ever takes that chair away, though all of us on the road see it.

"And I remembered when I first started seeing the chair, it was in the summer, in a field filled with little white flowers."

Yes. All of it now coming back to me. A field of little white flowers.

Billy was done. He had been shouting the whole thing to me. He looked out over the club; for a brief moment, it had dropped into shadow.

He turned and smiled at me, a little weary from the shouting. "It's such a pretty-hearted thing to do."

"Pretty-hearted," I said back to him. I liked that. I took a drink.

"And then—I don't even need to know who it is. It makes you less lonely, all the pretty-hearted things that strangers do."

Billy was a good old hippie. He found me and liked me and was very loyal. He wanted to share his moments and remind himself that we were more than just jobs and cars and families and drugs. It seemed he had given up on most of those things anyway, as I threaded together from random comments he had made since I met him. Billy wanted to share these moments and hear some in return, echoing each other, like a single thought across two minds. Once in a while he had a miss—he spent one long, drunk night describing his conversation with the moon—okay Billy, go home—but I liked his urgency.

But Billy was hard on his family, though; he didn't give details, but he said they were small-minded people. I worried that he betrayed them because I think he had kids. I thought he had mentioned it once, but I never asked about it. I knew he had had a wife, in the past tense. It was a struggle to understand how such a soft-hearted hippie would harbour those feelings toward his own. But we didn't talk about that stuff—instead, yellow chairs, the moon.

My phone vibrated. What? I pulled it out of my pocket.

Hey forgot to text earlier, we doing lunch tomorrow? It was Stasi.

I looked at the time. *Yeah of course.*

Then: *You still up?*

There was a pause.

Yeah up late sometimes.

Then: *See you tomorrow.*

I put the phone away.

"Who was that?" Billy asked.

"Sister," I said. "I'm seeing her tomorrow."

"Tell her to come out now." He grinned.

I had told Billy my stories too. I had described Convertible Corner and I think he got it—our awkward little grasps at happiness. I told him about relearning to breathe with the trumpet and he had loved that; he loved hearing how manipulating the clutch of my chest and push of my mouth could produce liquid amber emotion, a gold-plated sigh, a honeyed whine. He loved music of course, the trumpet in particular because he knew me; sometimes I thought he loved that I had no ambition with it. He was that type of guy.

"We just going to watch or what?" I gestured at the dancing crowd.

"Old man at the party," Billy said. Then, putting his arms up in the air, louder: "Old man at the party!"

We dumped our glasses and got lost in the crowd. I didn't see where Billy went, only the hands raised in the air as they disappeared among other hands, flapping palms and dancing fingers. Billy danced weird, but nobody bothered him about it: arms swinging, steps out of step, bouncy jumps with his head up. I faced the DJ with my hands in the air, calling down something exquisite. She laid out something smooth. A low tide pulled us out.

I felt cheap and happy. Cheap because none of this was real, happy anyway. It wasn't real without the drinking and the drugs; it was an elaborate, constructed kaleidoscope, a fantasy with occasional vomiting. Happy because the music was so loud I was lost in it, and the crowd so chaotic I disappeared. I didn't have to be ethical in my pursuit of a moment like this. Everyone else was ridiculous too—some people went to amusement parks, strapping into a machine that pulled them hundreds of feet into the air and shook them left and right. A shakedown of stress hormones, bored humans trying to come to life. Cheap and happy.

Alex circled through my vision and out again; she didn't see me. I didn't wave to her. Billy was gone. In front of me a man with long hair tilted his head back and started running his hands through it. His arms were thick out of his sleeveless shirt. His gestures were private, lost in himself.

I went back for another drink. The crowd was thinner at the bar now, all the tables were full, phone screens flickered. Waiting, I looked around. I wondered whether to go to the bathroom again or step outside for another joint to pass by. I pulled out my phone, but Stasi hadn't sent anything else. It was almost two in the morning, why would she be awake and texting me about lunch? I knew she got up early every day, running, whittling herself down. Lean as an arrow, piercing the skin of this world and finding herself in the wound. Something like that. That was her thing. I was drunk, but when my drink arrived I drained it, neat, clean, quick.

I didn't see Billy anywhere. I thought I recognized a few others, Wednesday regulars like us, off-night off-beat characters. None of the faces stuck. I weighed it again—I would go outside. I wanted to sleep tonight, I had that lunch tomorrow before my shift, another trip to the bathroom wouldn't make those things easier.

I stepped outside on the patio. It was cold but it did not bother me; my body accepted it without comment. I looked up briefly at the near-black sky and its fine dance of lights. I looked around and saw the groups of people; I picked three women sitting together, all leaning back on the benches and looking distant, rarely noticing each other except to lift an arm and pass a joint around. They looked like that Renaissance painting, women seated in various postures of repose. I sat with them and they all lifted their eyes to me, curious. None of them were young; they didn't have that blinking enthusiasm. They weren't trying to record everything. I turned and faced them. The bouncer was turned away, so I pulled out the baggie and put it on the bench next to my leg, pointing at the white square.

"Trade? If I can sit with that for a minute." And I nodded at the joint.

The woman closest to me had amber hair chopped at her chin and a faraway calm in her reddened eyes. The eyes themselves were lined all around in blue. She looked down at the square and smiled at it, then at me. Her friends leaned forward and looked down at the bench beside my leg.

"You can finish it," the nearest woman said, handing me the second half of a thick joint.

I leaned back into the bench. It was cold, but my body accepted it again. The woman plucked the square and put it into her pocket. Now the women were curious and amused by me; they all watched as I pulled on the joint, using my exhaustively trained mouth to blow an identical line of fading rings. They drifted sharp in the night air. Showing off in an innocent way, like a child—they accepted it simply as well.

"Who are you?" she asked.

I inhaled thoughtfully, I was high. I could have answered a million ways. I thought of my sister suddenly, her other names—Stasia, Stasi, even Stas. She had even tried Ana for a short while—her strong sense of self, her will to define and control it. It was tempting to be elaborate but at the last moment, I faltered; as always I was a child sitting in the sand, playing with sticks. I exhaled.

"I'm Peter, I guess," I said. "Anyway, that's what they named me when I was born." I rested the joint on my leg, red tip fading. "I never bothered to come up with anything else."

She was amused in her vague, big-eyed way. I started to notice things about her. I saw her long face as a carved wooden mask, drawn, detached from the inside, but with eyes showing everything. I started to feel sure of things—I felt she knew everything about me. I had split open, exposed like the jagged interiors of crushed fruit. This is how it felt sometimes, one inch deep on a second joint. I could be known just by someone looking at me; it was a relief, this idea I could be known, without the work. I could be seen, without asking. And another thing—that her knowing was not as witness to my life and its billions of tiny points, but instead because we were the same. And we both saw it. Knowing as a twin, as siblings, as children, the same flesh of one big soul, the same.

"So hi, Peter," she said.

"So who are you?" I asked.

Apparently she had not expected the question returned to her because her head tilted in genuine consideration. She paused on it, reflecting.

"I'm Zari, but that's not how they named me when I was born."

"Hi, Zari," I said.

The exchange made, she sat back and followed her own thoughts. I looked down and the joint was fading out.

"So we're the same then?" I asked, and after her eyes returned to me, I motioned for the lighter on the small table before her.

"What?" She handed the lighter over.

I wet my finger in my mouth and dampened the tip of the joint, running along the burned edge, then sparked it. It took the flame, reluctantly. "I mean, we're the same people then." I gave her the lighter back.

"How?" Her tone was rising, curious, and her friends were looking at us.

"I mean, we're the same people. Only we had different parents, different timing, different experiences growing up."

She winced slightly, and I could see in her tightened mouth that she was trying to determine if this made sense and she was too stoned to understand, or if I was stoned and not making sense. The truth is I had never thought it through very far or talked it out with myself. I had a feeling about it sometimes and normally I would think it out on my own—something real or a tunnel to nowhere?—but now, on this smoking patio behind the club, in the bitter black cold, I had just started talking. But her face told me it was a mistake.

"Well," she started slowly, again checking herself to see if she had missed it somehow. "Yeah. But parents, experiences, that's what makes you. That's who you are. That's genetics and, you know, childhood, so—" She stopped talking.

"Exactly," I said.

This quick agreement blanked her because she thought she was disagreeing. I finished the joint. She was staring at me. I was trying to hold on to the part of my mind that could verbalize properly, but I was rapidly approaching the cliff.

"So—" she started, unsure.

"So—we're the same people. We are the same except for parents, experiences."

She was suspicious of me now, and I knew it was a mistake, made no sense, I should not have wandered around with my lazy words and tilted mind. I don't even know why I pushed it again. I should break and run.

"Yeah," her friend said, the one sitting next to her. "He's right."

The two women looked at each other. I know the first woman was bothered that a stranger would offer anything in common, let alone that we were the same—it was too personal, too intrusive, it was not possible. Somehow I sensed that going in; I didn't know if I was picking an awkward fight, or why. The second woman, I couldn't read. But she was confident and simple with a wide-open face, long straight hair.

My hands were suddenly seizing, and I realized they were painful with cold.

"We're the same," the second woman said, standing up and stretching her back and arms. She showed no notice of the cold. "All of us. Same thing, just variations." The third woman, who hadn't spoken yet, also stood, and then the first one as well. They were leaving. "Pretty simple, actually," the second woman said as they filed around the small table. "Bye, Peter."

"Bye," I said, not looking at the first woman's face. I had walked into it stupidly, stoned, and did not want to see her eyes or mouth twisted in annoyance. Maybe they weren't, I didn't know. I waited until they went inside, dropping the end of the joint and grinding it into the ground, then standing up and going inside to be absorbed into the heat and noise of the club—the last ten minutes obliterated by the shock of this second world.

I looked around and didn't see Billy or Alex; it was late, I could just leave. The crowd was swaying, lights were arcing in a gentle half-spin across the ceiling and walls. I had an ending feeling in me. Everybody looked blurry, happy, and far away. I couldn't quite place the music or how it sounded, only how my body caved inward as the sound came outward, the exchange of it. I wanted to talk to Billy maybe, I should have asked him first—were people the same? I felt he could go either way. But I felt they were. I felt that believing people were the same was important to me, like a small red stone I wore around my neck.

I remembered a story Billy told about some photography he had done after leaving his career. He had bought an expensive camera, took photos of the streets, thoughtful portraits of strangers, but then he put up a website and had a few requests—would he shoot people's events for money? Sure, he tried a couple, they went okay. But the last one was some house party; a rich teen had several classes worth of kids over and wanted professional images of their epic night, a crowning jewel for extensive online personas, permanent records of greatness. Billy's words. So he showed up and walked around and saw a bunch of kids getting drunk, and whenever he entered a room with the camera they all exploded in postures of adulthood, the boys loud and goading, the girls jutting their chins up, everyone thinking the camera was focused on them. Billy got depressed—a middle-aged man with a gut, and having just left the corporate world for somewhat related reasons. He brought the camera up to his eye and pretended to shoot, and after about barely an hour and a half, all the kids were too wasted to notice he had located a large bottle of expensive cognac from the father's wood-panelled study and just fucked off home. Kids were allowed to be dumb, he reasoned, but he didn't have to participate. He had taken no photos. Later, when the girl contacted him for her photos, Billy gathered up 250 images he had found online and sent them to her—250 pictures of squirrels. Jumping, hiding nuts, sitting on tree branches, clinging to tree trunks, staring at the camera with their blank black eyes, grey and brown and red ones. Fucking. Squirrels. She flipped out, threatened him, threatened to get her dad to do something legal to him. Billy reasoned the father would be uninterested at best—that type of parent seemed like the kind to produce this type of girl. And he was right. No rich dad ever came crashing into his life with lawsuits or anything else. Billy was done with paid gigs, though.

Would he think people were the same? Those kids, and whoever was sitting in the yellow chair in an empty field? I thought Billy would say no. But I could also see that he would say yes. The hippie in him. He would have noticed the shy kids who winced and turned away when he walked in with the camera. In the other kids, he must have seen vanity as the hard, thin shell that it was—protecting something vulnerable and unformed. And I knew how invigorated he was by strangers, new people, endless sources of new recognition and understanding—there had to be something beyond who your parents were, and the enormous but tiny personal cosmos of things that had happened to you. Maybe none of that mattered—the only things we knew about ourselves, they didn't even matter.

I didn't see Billy around. Or anybody else I knew. My body was tired and confused, both up and down, my mind mostly down.

I went for my coat and called a ride, standing near the front of the club, remembering so many rides home in a silent car through empty streets, lulled into another ending with smooth rights and lefts, street lamps and headlights blurred into lines. And then I would be home, familiar and alone, and into bed, alone and familiar. It was an important ritual for me, after this one. The ride home and the bed.

I got my coat back and, as the throbbing music receded behind me, stepped out into the night.

EARLY NOVEMBER

I ATTENDED the meetings and looked around at circles of turtles. Sara and I had done our one-on-one chat, that quick necessary thing between a winner and a loser, acknowledging what had happened and confirming our willingness to ignore it in our future interactions. She must have known—with any shadow of intelligence she may have possessed in that expensively educated mind—that I had been screwed.

We made women's and men's apparel, mostly women's. Our men's collection was half-heartedly launched and frankly uninspired, more of an add-on for our female customers who, while shopping for themselves, charitably thought to pick up something for their partners too. Lazy in concept and execution, our men's line was never really our focus, and the sales showed it. We were started twenty years ago by a petite wisp of a woman, an artist who printed her own fabrics and started selling shift dresses. She had a keen eye for pattern and the instinct of a seamstress for flattering cuts. I was just out of school and joined her for sales and marketing when it was barely a full-time role. Everything blew up three years later when we landed our first national retailer. We hired sewers and kept production local, and that angle was a hit at the exact moment the market was asking for it. The artist had a musician friend; we made her a dress for her album cover and it was a breakout record—another bump for us. When an imitator showed up with similar patterns, we knew our narrative was pushing the market now.

But we blew up again when I pushed for patterned handbags and that, right there, was my ownership on the VP role. The artist had sold the company, we had new owners, and Sara was a well-bred corporate player who had just jumped from one big company to another; she never worked from the artist's basement, she didn't drive out samples. Her face was too smooth for her age, and I sensed manipulation in her, a cool blood, an eerie absence of any human anima. A showpiece, fine. Private school, MBA, with a WASPy last name. They bought her like a horse.

I ate lunch in my car, sometimes vegetarian food and sometimes a burger or shawarma; I knew eating meat was not the worst thing I did, and it was an occasional, greasy pleasure. Primal—accessing a private satisfaction I knew nowhere else. I started gaining weight but I lengthened my runs, waking up earlier, changing my alarm but not telling Christopher—I gained a bit of muscle. I still looked good but resented my body in the mirror, betrayed by how truthful it was about itself, showing everything. The physical life does not lie; bodies were the last honest things. You only had to learn how to read them.

Sarah had a mean teacher at school and that was taking up some time. She was anxious in the evenings, thinking of school in the morning. Sleep was getting hard. Sunday night was a wreck. I knew all this already—the brittle and tenuous connection to life, easily broken and betrayed, her fineness and open eyes and ears and skin and heart processing the world. Me, Peter, Mom, Grandpa. We all lined up for our whipping by the shouting beauty and tender traumas of life. All of us so sensitive, and now this beautiful girl, with soft brown hair that was shot with gold in the sun. Another one of us starting to stumble. I could find that teacher and crush him with my car, in deep and sudden spurts, back and forth, as I imagined vividly many nights—or I could let him tell the truth to my daughter: the world was cruel.

And I carried that knowledge for her, waiting. The world was cruel. I had to watch my daughter find it herself, and the weight of that guilt or helplessness or complete and airless inevitability was a whole new body, one with its own energy, its own movement in my life. All of us so sensitive, almost dying of it. All of us moving through this sleepwalker life, fully awake.

Christopher was out in the yard. He was wearing a cotton shirt, but it was cold outside. He was never cold, his slim figure ran on a hot current of energy. It was bright outside, the sun low in the sky, and sometimes I thought he took in some of that light through his fair skin.

"The lasagna tonight? It's easy," I said.

He turned around. "Yeah that sounds great."

"I'll put it in."

I went back in the house and got the box from the freezer, opened it, removed the plastic film, checked the box for the temperature, then slid the lasagna into the oven before it had started to preheat. One of those vegetarian ones with zucchini in it, weeknight cuisine in a domestic, child-rearing environment. Sarah was in the living room in front of the TV. I went to my purse and rummaged to the back, through the lining; I pulled out the phone, walked to the bathroom, locked the door, and turned on the phone, waiting for it to start up. I waited another two minutes, breathing. Nothing came in. I turned it off again.

I came out and slipped the phone back into my bag. That was my last chance to check tonight and there was nothing. The night ahead took on a different colour, but I was used to it, I would adjust—this was, after all, everyone else's life. No messages from the outside world.

I went back to the yard where Christopher was finishing his gardening, pruning and bundling up some of the bushes, his bare hands going pink, his breath lifting into the air, silver when it hit the sun. It was very pretty out. There was a quality to the air and light; my thoughts drifted back to Mateo, lazily, dreamily, seeking a small spark of arousal. But I closed it quickly. You had to close them quickly or they eroded everything else. You had to find a way to survive all the rest of life; there was so much of it.

The lasagna was not very good—we finished it quickly. Outside the windows, it was already dark; night was coming faster and faster now.

We put on an educational show about marine life, and I slipped outside to have a cigarette. Instead of remembering a coat, I had grabbed a throw blanket from the sofa and, struggling briefly, threw it across the back of my shoulders. I smoked like that, with the thick blanket across me, a ridiculous mane. The door opened and closed, and Christopher came out—I bristled, caught.

"Well," he said. "Found you."

I didn't say anything at first. He had put on a coat to come out.

"Sarah probably knows too," I said.

He didn't say anything to that. His hands were hidden in his coat pockets. "How is therapy going? We don't talk about that much."

"That's true," I said. "We don't. It's going okay, I think." He could have said something about the throw blanket across my shoulders but he was choosing the serious moment. "I was so angry at first and I wanted to control it, so it didn't get worse. I wanted to talk it out."

"You gave a lot of years to that company. A lot of weekends."

"Yeah, Sarah's youngest years too. We were really taking off—we were landing national retailers, had to triple production. I built that company. The founder had zero business skills, she was an artist, she sold quickly."

"I remember."

I took another pull and exhaled. "But now it's mostly about family. Mom, Dad, Peter. I guess therapy usually goes that way. Can't seem to quit the cigarettes, though."

"It doesn't matter."

The black November night crowded in, dense and cold, filled with little stars.

He was quiet as I smoked. Then: "Sarah knows."

"The smoking?" I said quickly.

"Yeah."

"Is she upset about it?"

"She gets stressed about you getting sick," he said. "She hears about them being bad for your health."

I tapped out the cigarette against the side of the house and watched the ember shatter and fall. "So she talked to you about it."

"She asked me once."

I put the butt in the outside garbage bin. The lid clattered loudly as I dropped it. I remembered it could be heard from inside the house. I privately cursed myself.

"Go in?" I asked.

"Yeah sure."

Sarah was still in the TV room; Christopher joined her. I went to the bathroom to brush my teeth. I kept a second brush in the downstairs bathroom now, little habits, little rituals around the bad thing I was doing. Performing so many actions to dance around it. And not understanding their meaning—was Sarah bothered by me smoking? Maybe. Did it matter? Maybe not. These selves of mother and wife taking on new postures that had nothing to do with me, instead a hiding of me. This weight of two lives on top of my own. This hiding, this distance.

Christopher had left his coat on the chair near the door. I hung it up carefully in the closet, adjusting the arms on the hanger, zipping it up partially so it took its shape.

When I came back into the TV room, I saw them for a brief moment before they saw me; I saw their mute staring, faces lit up by the television. That's always an odd, arresting moment, watching people watch TV—you don't recognize them at first. And when you do, they seem far away.

***

My phone rang—I hit the button quickly.

"What's up, Sonya? I'm driving, you're on speaker."

Monday morning. I was driving out to a large, well-kept boutique in the suburbs where we weren't selling well. I wanted to see their display. I could make recommendations. I also wanted to meet the new owner.

"Oh, okay. Actually I was following up on the email about the Dalton samples—they are asking."

"Right. Can you throw that in an email again and attach the pricing?"

"Sure. They are asking because they have capacity next month."

"Yes, I remember, but can you throw it in an email again? Attach the pricing. I'll get to it."

"Great. I will. Yeah, they just emailed me today."

"No problem, Sonya, I'll get to it. I'm in the car right now so just toss it back to me."

"Okay no problem."

"Perfect, thank you. Bye, Sonya."

"Bye," she said.

I hit the button.

Sonya. Detail-oriented but fretful. Struggled to move projects forward. Young, though. She just needed to make some minor mistakes, own it and get over it, and then release her brain from the hesitation.

I was sitting on the highway and we were crawling, rolling in and out of stops. The valley dipped wide and away on either side of the road, deep with the colour of cool grass, a colour that made me remember the feel of it under my feet.

I let myself imagine it. I could pull over onto the shoulder and get out of the car. I could climb over the barrier and drop onto the ground. I could take off my shoes and walk out into the valley. I would get smaller and smaller until I was somewhere out there in the middle green. Out there I could turn around and look at the cars, their colourful turtleback tops glittering in the sun. And the cars would look at me, each of us so innocently convinced the other was absurd.

But in one car there would be a man, a different one, and he would look ahead at the cars and then turn to look at me, then the cars again and then me. And he would pull over and get out, drop to the ground, walking out; he would stride through the grass slowly at first, as if considering, willing to change his mind. But alone in the deepening green he would be sure.

I thought of Isabelle suddenly. She interrupted me sometimes, the memory of her saying, "And what did that mean to you?" She stressed the last word. She had asked it more than once, suggesting something to me that I had not considered before—that something could have two meanings. Its own, separate—and one for me. "What did that mean to you?"

And yet I was quitting with her.

I didn't tell her I was stopping therapy, I just said I was taking a break, and she said of course; I imagine this was how people often phrased it, not wanting to admit defeat. It had been a whim, a message I sent, sitting alone in the car that was increasingly becoming some kind of not-work, not-home, not-Mateo reality. But it felt right in that moment, as if I had been cornered and was fighting to get free.

Our last session, she had asked me about sex as if it was a transactional game, with rules, objects: did I explore with Christopher? The question revealed how far apart we were, Isabelle and I. Sex was meaningless, an expression of an otherwise inexpressible thing—not about sex at all, but the only language was sex itself. I could not even comprehend that myself but I knew when something was stupid, and her question was stupid. Did I explore with Christopher? My whole life was Christopher. No, I did not explore with Christopher, it was absurd; I carried him and cared for him and my body was silent. And he did the same. It was a mistake to think acts and people were interchangeable—that I should eat zucchini lasagna with Mateo, that I should worship Christopher. So I had ended it with her a few days later. I felt, somewhere ahead of us, we would start excising Mateo from my life; that's where she wanted me to go.

But once I knew I was releasing her, my hostility dwindled. I didn't resent that wall of certificates anymore—I don't know why I ever did. Maybe I was afraid of some upper hand, my arrogance bristling as always.

I wondered, briefly, if she knew that, if maybe I was a "type" and she saw me, understood me behind that blankness—I was the person coming to therapy without wanting to change. After I ended it, maybe I even liked Isabelle and would miss some things about her. I thought, the things people tell her, they tell nobody else in the world—ever, even until death. And I wondered what was required to absorb that intimacy over a lifetime; it was work, with strangers, for money. And she was there trying to help.

I looked in the rear-view, remembering when Sarah was younger and sat in a carseat, I would see her face tilted to the side, looking out the open windows, hair whipping across her cheeks and eyes. I looked at her a lot, without her knowing. It was the best time to look at children, when they didn't know—the best time to look at most people, actually, to understand them as they are. But not Mateo. Whether you were looking at him or not did not matter, he would be the same, he was untouched that way by other people.

Alone in the car, all I could see in the rear-view was the car behind me, crawling along as I did.

When I sent the message to Isabelle saying I was taking a break from therapy and she responded less than five minutes later—*Of course, no problem*—I felt that dart of regret.

She didn't ask why. When you let someone go and they make it easy for you, you don't feel relieved—you feel a bit sick and close the phone quickly, you go into the kitchen and preheat the oven, you forget what you were going to put in. I had felt cornered, but now the walls were off and I was adrift. And it felt familiar. It was not the first time I had lost someone that way.

On the highway, we were still in the crawl.

So much time.

I've seen the "life wisdom" articles—they tell you to pretend you're talking to your younger self. What would you say? What would you tell yourself ten years ago? The only thing that seemed less and less true was time; the only thing I would tell myself is not to believe life is short, because in fact it is not, in fact it is very long, sitting in cars looking out into valleys, waiting in lineups and lobbies, standing in front of microwaves in office kitchens, watching circular meetings spin for hours. Life was unbearably long. And yet I would tell my younger self: it was still so short. I lost years—years. I lost years working, trying to win something, own something, or have something own me. Because I could not live without ownership. Belonging, in a final way. Life was so short, it walked away when you weren't looking, it was bored of you. I lost years and could not believe it, yet I sat on highways without moving—I had so much time. And I was losing years.

Belonging, ownership—yet always battling an instinct to escape. Why couldn't Isabelle see that? And if she did, why didn't she help?

I gained a car length, two.

It didn't matter.

Ultimately I knew I had been asking Isabelle for what she could not do: offer me insight not about myself but about life, the immense and heartbreaking noise of it, trying to turn that noise into something closer to song. I wasn't religious. And philosophers—they were all men from hundreds of years ago. I wanted a woman to tell me what all this was, a woman in her forties or older, lusty and angry and newly unafraid. Out of the great hollow chest of complacency, a wild and panicked heart was trying to beat free, escape, end up where it didn't belong—vulnerable and damaged and yet certain that suffering had worth.

Break things open, burn them, turn over stones, split trees, watch the storm come in and bring everything down on your head and ears and eyes tightly shut. Know this life that way.

Cars ahead were moving out of the crawl. Slowly we gathered speed, starting to space ourselves out, the white lines between lanes getting faster and shorter.

A lane ahead was clear. I snapped the pedal down and darted into it, then into the next space ahead—and then two more times.

Then I stayed where I was, following the pace around me. Lulled, quieting. Falling back in with everyone else.

* * *

He was pulling off his coat, not looking at me from under his heavy brow. Snow had caught in his hair and he brushed his hand lightly across it; flakes shook loose and fell until they disappeared. "Snowing," he said.

"Seems early this year," I said, watching him from the chair beside the bed. I kept my face still although my blood was already quick.

"November's not so early." He dragged his boots off.

Finally he looked up and his face changed, became alert. "What? What's on your mind?"

"How about a shower?"

His eyes blinked slowly, dreamily, into a smile that showed last in his mouth. "Ah, so it's like that tonight."

"Your favourite," I said.

"My favourite? Your favourite," he said—laughing eyes, soft voice. Sometimes I amused him when I was being serious. I was always serious.

We went into the dark bathroom, and I lit a short candle on the sink, then lit my cigarette on the darting, gold flame. I sat on the seat of the toilet, knees apart, taking a slow pull.

"You can't smoke in here," he said in a tender voice.

"It's okay, it's just a fine, I'll pay," I said. "You start."

He kept smiling and repressing it; that withholding lit something in my blood, a scent, a chase.

He pulled his sweater over, his T-shirt underneath. He undid his belt and slid his pants down. He stood in tight shorts in the half-darkness, looking down at me with heavy-lidded eyes under that heavy brow, scratching his chest. The candle lay orange lines across his legs, his chest, his blunt profile. "Can I?" He motioned for the cigarette. I handed it over and he took a drag the way non-smokers sometimes do, wincing, too deep. "Terrible," he said, handing it back.

"You smoked when you were younger," I said.

"I did many terrible things when I was younger," he said. He turned on the shower, running his hand through the stream, waiting for heat. He slipped his shorts down.

He stepped into the shower, faced the stream, and tipped his head forward into it; the water collected in his hair and rolled down his face and neck and shoulders, down the front of his body. In the white-tiled stall, candlelit, he looked darkly bronze; the fading summer tan of his thick limbs, the untouched creamy white of his chest and thighs. The cigarette glowed and faded as it moved from my mouth to my hand. He rubbed his face in the water, knowing something I never had to tell him: to move slowly, to spend a single moment as if it were two. He turned around and kept his head lowered, letting the water run down his shoulders and back in warm rivers. He was good about this, and I never had to tell him. He understood what it was about. Slowness, heat.

I finished the cigarette and slipped it under the seat, then slipped out of my clothes, down to underwear. I took a washcloth from the rack and sat on the edge of the bathtub, dipping the cloth into the water, squeezing it and letting it go and turning it over.

He ignored this, still rubbing his face in the water, facing away, the water rolling over his face from behind, closing his eyes.

"The wall," I said. He turned and faced the wall, and then, relaxing, he leaned onto it with his elbows and forearms, resting; after a moment he leaned his head against his arms. He was prostrate, resting on the wall, his face turned in profile.

With the washcloth wet, I started on his feet, the heels and ankles, rubbing in soft circles around them. I tugged on his left foot, and he lifted it for me gently. I dug into his heavy heel, gripped his ankle between both hands, gripped that naked tendon, thick as steel cable. I bent low over his feet, first one and then the next. He lifted them, leaving their weight full. I heard the parables, knew the religions, the popes bending to wash the feet of the homeless, the poor and the dying, that terrifying intimacy between strangers, the heartbreaking hope of it, the tears jumping to your eyes. Dogs with rib cages showing. The water ran down my arms; I moved in circles, firm.

I moved up his calves, dense muscle like stone, and pulled on them, circled them, moved the cloth around to the front and back. Low columns, I gripped each in both hands. I was waking up, stirring. Feeling a movement, something meditative, like worship, a movement in the blood that drew the mind far away. His muscles released. I looked up. His body rose up above me, monstrous in the dim room, his shoulders slack, resting on the wall, his head turned to the side. All I could see was the chest gently moving. I circled his knees with the wet cloth and held them, tight, bracing. Softer, I squeezed behind them, the pulling reflex behind his knee, caving his strength for a breath, for two. Water ran down my face and neck, shoulders and arms.

I moved up to his thighs. Looser than his calves but springing back with elastic power when I pressed the muscle between my hands. I kneaded into them from behind, feeling muscles tense and let go. Immense power, inert, waiting. When I looked up now, his body was newly naked, falling, wet, into sleep. I circled the cloth around, to the front of his thighs, pulling heavily down, dragging his strength past his knees, pulling him lower, weaker. The beginning of his hips, caving. I pulled on the front of his thighs until I felt him slowly loosen, unable to hold himself up. I was enveloped now by the water running down the front of my body.

I stood up. I was almost as tall as him, but he was twice my width, his back wide and sloping at the shoulders. Nobody else would understand this, but he did, quietly accepting. In his giving over. In that he did not talk or look at me. He faced the wall, rested on it with his bulky, faded-sun arms, laid his head down. A gift of pure, wordless freedom—weightless—not having to talk, not searching around, not asking to see my disappointments or boredom, my arrogance or isolation, not asking to examine them. I never told him any of that, I never gave him rules. In that silence I was, at last, fully gone.

I rubbed his back, the centre column of his body, from the top moving down, down moving up. I moved in heavy strokes across his ribs. I gathered the cloth in my hand, pushing its roughness into him, dragging it across him. I put the cloth aside and smoothed the skin again with bare palms: lazy, dream-heavy. He was receding into a grey fog outside this room—I was present now with a slumbering, distant animal, a silent body. That broad back and thick legs. That round, dark head dipped between the shoulders. The edge of his jaw. His darkened arms and white chest. I leaned forward and brushed my lips between his shoulders.

I sat down on the edge of the bathtub and massaged the top of his thighs again, gripping each one with both hands, slipping briefly between his legs. I moved from one thigh to the other, finding a rhythm with it, a pulse. I leaned forward and bit firmly into the muscle, my jaw tightening quickly, then softly releasing; I heard him make a sound—not of pain, but of suppressing pain. I was falling behind the same fog, losing myself, disappearing into a rhythm, into worship. Absented, I parted with my self and left that noise behind. And he was so far away—the only intimacy I could know, one of distance. I found my voice was almost gone and I struggled to clear the words, "Turn around."

THURSDAY

I WOKE halfway to awake, last night's sounds echoing in a dim and narrow space behind my eyes. I was in bed, wearing pants and nothing else, one of those poor decisions you made when you were younger. I started kicking off the blankets but my body whimpered, so I stopped. I still had a bit of time.

The first thing my mind would want to do is start replaying small scenes and something I had said, but I knew I would be embarrassed somehow, it never failed, I was never quite who I wanted to be, even lost in a group while perked up and mellowed out. I did see both Billy and Alex, which made me feel good and often would last through the week. They were strange friends from a very specific place—I felt that way about people from work too. I had put a glass of water on my bedside table last night—that was smarter, it made up for the pants—and I sat up and drank about half of it. I lay back down.

I was meeting Stasi for lunch but I had some time. I liked the diner but it wasn't the type of place my sister would know; it was inexpensive, though. I knew Stasi would offer to pay and of course I would accept, it was foolish to do otherwise, but I liked knowing it would not be a big dent for her.

Face up, I thought about the next few hours. Stasi. Anastasia. Protective, blunt, responsible for everyone all the time. Tall like our father. I sat up and finished the water by my bed, the glass coming down heavily on the table, my body still working to get the arms and legs right. But I got my pants off, kicking, and stayed in bed for another twenty minutes.

I showered and put on my clothes, nicer ones, and put on the shoes I wore to the audition. I made a half-hearted attempt at coffee, a dismal, brown thing. I drank it all. I had never got good at coffee. I brought a large bottle of water to the table and sat on the sofa in front of it, putting my phone on the table face up so I could see the time. Shoes already on, I had a little over half an hour before I had to leave. Outside the window, it was snowing. My head felt thick and chewed out but still somehow alive, sparking—leftover sparks from the night before, flaring and fading out. If I had some of that joint now—but not before lunch.

I remembered Stasi had texted me last night; why message so late? I looked at my phone's empty face—it was time to go.

The thick, light snow wandered around instead of falling straight down. Pretty. Not in a hurry, not much of a life for snow; once you're on the ground, it's over. Most of it melted as it touched down and the sidewalks were wet with it, black. I came up along the window of the diner and glimpsed Stasi sitting there, looking sharp in her tight-shouldered blazer with her thick, ombré hair falling heavily down her chest.

Stasi always looked like she was at a job interview. She was almost grim about how she dressed, she wanted to be intimidating, she equated that with respect. But always with that rich ombré hair, as if she couldn't pick just one colour, she had to have both. I remembered suddenly I was still hungover and hoped I didn't look rough; I had dressed nicely, I hoped it was enough.

Stasi saw me and smiled big. It flooded through me like heat. She liked me, she really did. We saw the world so differently—it was hard to clash against each other's hard parts; one of us would always be soft. And we had learned an easiness with each other over the years. She waved me over as I came inside. I felt good suddenly, seeing her smiling, seeing another strange friend from a very specific place.

We both got minestrone soup and talked a bit. Stasi was in a bright mood but seemed distant behind that brightness, like a shield. The conversation coasted along the surface, and we hit some of the usual beats: she liked to ask about me getting online and I liked to say no. It was an old habit; years ago, she had lectured me seriously about having a presence, as a musician, but I'd asked about her own online brand and it fell apart into joking. She liked to wag her finger at me, that was all.

At one point we talked about vices, but she shut down quickly when I said something vulnerable; she avoided that in general. I had said something vague about getting lost with a crowd, feeling as if we were all together in some shared thing, seeing others as the same—she didn't like that. Shut the door quick.

Honestly, I was too hungover to make much more of our lunch anyway, but she did say something about her head getting kicked in—she'd lost a promotion at work—so I knew she wasn't entirely dormant for the season. When she talked like that, her guard was down. And she had tried therapy, she said. Her eyes jumped all around when she mentioned that. And she smelled of smoke.

The diner was quiet but the server was tired, I could tell, waiting for the shift to end. I knew those days. The server looked at the big clock behind the counter, then outside. I told Stasi I couldn't pay her back the money she had lent me last year, but she brushed it aside, as she had done before. I told her about the audition, and I knew if I got it, I would have the money next time. "At least you didn't forget the trumpet," she said at some point, joking around, and I knew she meant nothing by it, but actually it was a jolt backward—something I hadn't thought about for a long time. It moved to the back of my mind, waiting there.

She gave me a lift home and offered me a cigarette that sent my hangover shuddering through my body; I threw the smoke out the window. I forgot how much she enjoyed punishment. Driving through the slow-moving snow was peaceful, though, and I realized she hadn't mentioned Christopher or Sarah during the lunch. I thought of asking about them but passed, looking out the window instead.

I liked Christopher, he seemed frictionless as a husband, good for Stasi, and Sarah was shy and mature, preferring to be around adults but not talking much. It seemed exactly the type of family to assemble around my sister and her commanding posture in the world; they wouldn't crowd her and ask too much. Stasi said something about Christmas as she dropped me off, light and casual, but I knew I wouldn't go—I felt she knew that too—and I climbed up the stairs to my place, suddenly heavy, and started to pull off my nicer clothes as soon as I got in the door. I hung everything carefully in my closet, then went to the window and tilted my face along the glass, looking down at her car. She was still sitting there with the engine on.

I went to the bathroom and splashed my face with warm water, looking at my cheeks and eyes and nose, everything a little pink and tired. I got more water from the kitchen sink and thought of Stasi again, going to the window and looking out. She was still there. I waited a few minutes, looking down at her car. Her hands suddenly showed up on the wheel and she peeled out, sharply, and with a sudden heave of speed she was gone in the opposite direction. Stasi had a nice car, the kind that tempted you for a little speed, a tiny high.

I lightly packed the pipe, got stoned, and went back to bed and crawled under the covers. I knew I had almost a full hour and a half between the lunch and leaving for my night shift. An hour and a half felt like a delirious decadence I could barely comprehend—me, a mere recovering mortal among the languid hours where angels live, where they roll infinitely tangled with each other in warm, supple beds—I pulled the covers up to my chest and fell in and out of a hungry, heavy sleep.

It didn't last an hour. I kept waking up as a dream was winding down. The dreams were little more than frustrating mazes of mixed ideas, but I still felt as if important things were happening. But they weren't, they never were.

I sat up in bed and looked at my phone; I had to get dressed and leave for work. Getting out of bed, I didn't feel high but I didn't feel sober either, starting to remember the lunch, and Stasi, already looking it over in the past tense—it felt like yesterday. I put myself together and got my heavier coat for work, stepping outside with it zipped to the top of my neck and a hat pulled low over my ears.

I wasn't awake for much of the commute, not awake in the way you usually think of it—looking and listening around you. I was inside my coat, mostly. Warm and alone with my thoughts. What Stasi had said—forgetting the trumpet. I brought it back in my mind and fell into the memories, invisible in my coat and no one looking at me, safe among strangers.

The thing was, I had realized what I had done almost immediately.

It was more than ten years ago now. I was going to an audition and I was taking Grandpa's trumpet as a kind of totem, trying to borrow meaning from his life, a charm of luck for this small thing I wanted. I had a newer instrument already; this was for him. And I was on the subway lost in my thoughts, just anxious circles, imagining every fatal scenario from the auditions that haunted me, and my stop came, and I got up and left. There was no delay after the subway doors had closed behind me—the sound jolting my mind backward, back to the trumpet case on the floor next to the seats.

These things happen in slow motion. That's how you remember them later. I was turning around as the train lurched forward and slid along the platform, gaining momentum slowly and heavily.

The next few hours I do not remember as well, except as a staccato of panic and cold fear. I remember the aching chest and stomach. I went to the station bathroom, hot sweat in patches all over my body, but I shivered uncontrollably. I went to the booth and told the transit staff, they got on the phone, then turned and looked at me—two of them, an older man and woman—and their faces were set as best they could, neutral and blank, public-servant faces, but I could see they really felt bad. They felt terrible for me. The trumpet was gone.

I did not go home. I stayed for an hour in the station within sight of the booth. There was nothing; they heard nothing. I left the station, surfacing on the street, swallowed into air and noise and passersby, the world glittering and cold around me—I was broken, devastated.

I had lost the trumpet.

I decided to walk home. It would be an hour and a half at least. I don't remember much of that walk either, except moving along the blur of streets, wearing my black clothes and shoes. I can't remember what I thought—how to explain to the people at the audition, what to say to Mom—or whether my mind spiralled into blankness and died there. It was probably a shattered assembly of all of it; I remembered the fear and the failure, all the failure. Yet I knew my family would not be so surprised: this was who I was. There would be shock, but not surprise. I was fulfilling myself, a forgetful young man nervous on the train, failing because of myself and not because of the trumpet or music or anyone else.

And, barely able to even consider the idea, the fleeting wonder: had I done this to myself? Subconscious sabotage—musicians don't forget their instruments. I had to look away.

Walking blind through the streets, I was passing through an intersection when I heard it.

There was something thin and high in the air. A park on the far corner was surrounded by office buildings on the other three sides; I was still downtown, the throb of traffic blunting most of what I could feel and hear. But it was piercing, above the street, somewhere above our heads. And that was the moment. At the end of my life I could forget everything else but I would not forget that. I looked up and the sun was breaking across the buildings and their smooth glass faces, as high and bright as the sound. Because of course I knew what it was.

I crossed the street twice toward the park and the sound. The fear had transformed now into something more urgent, more terrifying, a great loss suddenly ahead of me if I was wrong. I could not be wrong. I was in the park and I saw the man.

Along the grass were benches and I saw him sitting there with the twisted gold in his hands. As I approached, he was just lowering it—at his feet, the case.

I reached my stop; my memory faded out. A handful of people got off the train and I fell in line behind them; we ascended the escalators standing in dark, formless coats. I surfaced at the street and noticed the snow, it was starting to collect on top of everything.

It was a ten-minute walk to work, and I fell back into the memory.

The old man had looked up at me as I approached him, and when our eyes met he seemed to smile sadly. My face. I guessed he knew. I walked up to him and, heart trying to break free from my chest, I forced the words out: "Where did you get that trumpet?"

"It's yours, then?"

My voice suddenly failing, I nodded.

"I found it on the train," he said, considering my face. "So it's yours then."

"Yes, it's mine."

"It's nice, it's an older one and I recognize it." He rested it on his knee. "So here, sit down."

He did most of the talking because I was stricken with the loss and the find; it was not anything I had experienced in my life, nothing close. He was in the war, too. "My name is Ron but they called me Horse and I liked it," he said.

I told him briefly about Grandpa, pushing it through my closed throat, a man I did not know closely, intimately, as a man in his plainest heart, but I said he was in the war.

And he said, "Some of us fall in love with the trumpet."

His body was turning pink from sitting in parks in the sun, his skin was lined and thick, spotted over. He was very old, with long thin legs. I could see a tall, straight man when he was young.

"I'm sorry I put my mouth on it," he said. "I don't have a cold or anything, but I know you will clean it when you get home. Here you go." He put the trumpet back in its case and snapped it closed. "I thought, well, maybe someone will hear me playing. And you did. You found me." His face showed no surprise, as if anything in this life was possible. As if his faith in that was natural. He lifted the case to me, but I was still locked somehow, unable to move. "What's your name?"

"I'm Peter," I said, reaching for the case. Dumbstruck with its weight back in my hand, I left. And I had said barely anything to him.

I got to work, and the memory went dark. I went in through the back and pulled my heavy coat off onto the rack, feeling the enormous shell of warmth suddenly leave. Marc was not there and the back kitchen was empty. Stu was up on grill. I checked the schedule and confirmed I would start on prep. I washed my hands in the sink with steaming water and bright blue soap.

I pulled bulbs of garlic and bags of onion. I took a large, shining knife and started clearing the skins, remembering.

Horse was what they called him because he worked hard but did not complain; he was valuable, he was a horse. But he was injured early and sent home, did not see his friends die, but of course many of them did. Those who came back were ghosts. They went back to jobs and families as ghosts. And he saw them wherever he went but knew he had escaped out of pure luck. Dumb luck. As he had handed me the trumpet case, I felt cold. I knew I did not belong with the instrument anymore, nothing in my life would echo his—with my grandfather dead, I knew the trumpet belonged to him.

Stu came to the back, his apron snug around his waist and generously spattered. "Peter," he said. "Hey, man."

"Hey, Stu," I said.

"Looking rough."

"Do I?"

Stu grinned, again in a good mood, teasing, two shifts in a row. A Stu rainbow. "No, I'm just messing. You make it easy." He wanted to hang out and chat. "Did you go out last night?"

"Yeah, I had some drinks," I said. "Listened to music." I swept onion and garlic skins into the bin.

The order system dinged, and Stu went back out to the grill.

I sliced the onions and brought them to a large pot, coated them in oil and salt, moving them around to break them apart.

It was a moment and it passed. I should have given the trumpet to Horse and walked away, light and clean, blameless, with the only right thing happening between us. *Horse, you should have it. It doesn't belong to me. I have another trumpet because this is yours.* And I would walk away. It was clear and bright between us, the right thing to do, but the moment passed and I watched it go. And I had walked away.

The onions were smoking and sweetening in the black crust that formed.

Danielle came to the back with a tray of dishes, looking at me briefly as she grappled with the tray. She unloaded plates and platters into the sink. Danielle was in her mid-twenties and dyed her short hair blond. She wore thick-framed glasses in lime green, which ended up being the most notable thing about her; otherwise she was pleasant and modest and bland. It was as if someone else had bought the glasses and put them on her face.

"Hi, Danielle," I said. "Closing again tonight?"

"Yeah, I took the shift from Ange."

Danielle took her tray back out. I moved the onions around once more and went back to the garlic. I pulled two cloves tight together and let the blade fly through them.

That was it with the trumpet and the old man.

I had walked steadily away in the park and along the street and eventually down into the subway, everything smooth and automatic, the case in my hand.

It wasn't only that I hadn't given it to him. It was the reason why I hadn't. I was more afraid of the gesture, an intimacy with a stranger, offering a gift like that. I didn't think I would miss the trumpet—my new one, at significant expense, was better—it was that I was afraid. I was afraid of the intimacy. Afraid he might say no, or that I would embarrass myself.

I knew I had missed something, ruined it.

And when I had got home, I lied—several times, to different people. I told Mom I went to the audition and it went well, and a week later I said I didn't get the gig. I told Stasi and a few others I did not get to the audition; I had lost the trumpet on the train, but they found it at another station and I went and picked it up. I should have maintained the first lie and kept the rest to myself. I told nobody about Horse. And my grandfather's trumpet changed for me, forever—I didn't think of him, I thought of the old man in the park, a gift ungiven, and war.

I brushed the minced garlic into a small pile in the corner of the board and looked in on the onion, stirring once. Not yet.

Cruel, life-giving luck. Random, brutal luck. In war, you live, another dies, no reason. Like leaves falling from a tree, half of them fall into the sun, half into shade. How meaningless to be alive for no reason. I had never even been near a war; all I knew I had read or watched. A child, in a way, curious to understand. A little boy carrying that trumpet.

I had forgotten my apron. I got one from the hooks and tied it around my waist, standing up front near the grill as Stu moved around. He saw me tying a second knot on the apron strings, staring off. I was feeling kind of low with the memory. And hangovers sometimes pulled me down.

"It's been quiet for a Thursday," Stu said. "I got the mushrooms done early." I looked at my phone quickly—nothing.

"Okay, thanks Stu," I said, and went back to the kitchen.

Some of us fall in love with the trumpet—what did that mean? Trumpets were used in war, bugles too. I remembered the clarion, the highest register, a piercing call, nothing above it. A single high note. And the clarion call—bringing all together into one, a uniting, a mass belonging, all of us the same. Like what I said to Stasi—we didn't have anything like that anymore. What did it feel like? To get called to something big. Not alone but with so many others. To be, and feel, the same. We didn't really have anything big; we were all fractured off, little tribes of families or friends or half-friends, mostly online, mostly alone. We were singular and apart.

My thoughts returned to the kitchen. I preheated the oven. I cut the heat on the onions and dropped in the garlic, stirring as the hissing oil slowed and cooled and quieted. I pulled a tray of tomatoes from the rack and set it down by the sink, bringing the water to warm and starting to rinse the tomatoes between my hands. I was reaching the point when the hangover is less in the body and more in the mind, pulling and dragging things down. Me in a war? I could barely handle an audition or talking to a stranger; I'd be useless, especially as a teen, a "young man" with the face of a child. Whole generations of young men raised to never show weakness, never show emotion, then sent into hell. Some of us fall in love with the trumpet—why? War was hell. I trimmed and dressed the tomatoes and set them in rows on the tray but the oven wasn't ready. Instead I opened a few cans of sauce and waited, leaning against the counter, looking down at the floor.

I'd be the young soldier who ran out into the woods and froze to death. Or starved. Or found a farm, and the family there looked at me and wondered whether their lives were worth mine. And if they pitied my child's face and animal's fear and shit-stained uniform and offered me soup, a bed, if they were caught helping me, what would become of them? Shot, maybe. Better that I'd be the young soldier who ran away and shot himself.

Stu came to the back. "Just hanging out?"

I started. "Waiting for the oven."

The oven beeped immediately. I put the tomatoes in, closed the door, and set the timer. Stu was still standing there, so I felt I should keep talking. I was in a strange mood.

"Any beautiful moments lately?" I said to him, using Billy's thing.

Stu's mouth tightened. "What?"

"You know, beautiful moments."

"Moments like, during the day?"

"Yeah, just a random moment in your day. But beautiful."

Stu gave it genuine consideration. "Today?"

"Maybe not today, but recently. Something you remember."

Stu was staring, thinking. "A couple weeks back, a cashier was scanning a few things and she missed the six-pack. I don't think it was on purpose or anything, she just missed it. Put it in the bag, it was free."

"I remember that, you told me after. Not a bad haul." I went into the cooler to pull a few stems of herbs. In there I remembered the butter and lemon. I came out. "Is Marc coming in tonight, do you know?"

"I don't think so," Stu said. "He was here earlier, and I think he left for the night." He went back toward the grill but stopped just short of the doorway. "You? Anything happen to you?"

"Not recently, but a long time ago I lost my trumpet on the train and, as I walked home, I heard somebody playing it. In a park. And I found him and he gave it back to me."

"Are you serious?"

"Yeah."

"That's unbelievable."

"It was a long time ago, but I think about it sometimes."

"What are the chances of that?"

"Zero, I think. I don't think it's possible."

"I've never heard a story like that."

"I know, me neither."

Stu again turned to go to the grill but again stopped. "Hey, did they call you? The audition?"

A tall, heavy weight inside my chest tipped, lurching, as if to fall down. "Not yet."

"Okay, no problem, they will."

The timer hadn't gone off yet, but I stopped it with half a minute left and pulled the blackened tomatoes out. Seeing I was busy, Stu left. I added the tomatoes to the pot, and the sauce, and the butter; I upped the heat and stirred. Good now, time to walk away.

With Stasi, I could see it. Her ending up in therapy. I didn't know of any other rejection she'd had; I knew none of her disappointments. She had few failures, not because she was necessarily favoured her whole life but because of her control, her self-discipline. She was competent and aggressive in a way that didn't turn people off. And she was deeply sensitive, reading the room and people and finding her note in the balance. She was CEO of our family since we were kids, and sometimes I thought our father was intimidated by her—where did this little fire come from? Good at school and relationships, Stasi stayed with her first job as it rocketed up. I realized, at forty, this might have been the first time someone had told her no. It must be hard to get this far for that to be your first. Bewildered, as if reality had broken, she went to therapy.

I pulled some steaks and puffs out of the freezer for thawing and started a fresh pot.

But it may have been unkind of me to assume that of Stasi, and I didn't like to be unkind with her. I didn't know enough about her life. She would not have surprised me if she revealed dozens of disappointments over the years, it's possible she buried them all. She was hard like that. For all that sensitivity, she was not unlike Stu. That brusque relationship with the world was revealed in so many casual comments and unimportant moments as a bristling against some kind of hurt.

I poured myself a coffee. It was good and strong, and I was feeling better when my phone started vibrating.

I looked at the screen.

Now—it was happening now.

I started to try to finish my coffee quickly but gave up and, panicked, inexplicably and suddenly dumped the rest of it in the sink. I went quickly out the back two doors and outside the restaurant, beside the dumpsters and cigarette cans.

"Hello?"

"Is this Peter?"

"Yes, this is Peter."

"Hi Peter, it's Lucia."

And I knew. Her name, the way her voice fell slightly at the end. *It's Lu-cia*. It was cold outside and the green metal of the dumpster had been decaying into browns for years; behind it a small lot with rough-looking cars, lined by a chain-link fence on its slow way down. The backs of restaurants are some of the realest places on earth—just a door or two from your beautiful meal. It was cold and I hadn't brought my jacket.

"Hi, Lucia," I said, bright but failing.

"I'm calling about the audition." She paused. I remembered suddenly how low and dark her voice was.

I waited. Then I said quickly, "Yes, the audition."

"I really liked your performance, Peter."

Her voice again, falling at the end. But it was okay now,

better. My hangover was better and the coffee had warmed me, moved through me, and last night Alex had a friend and Billy bought me a drink. Everything was still okay in a lot of ways. I waited.

"We saw a couple of people and, you know, I thought you were great, but we did have another person—there was another person we picked."

As deep as her voice was, she was unsteady. I sensed the softness in her, and it responded in me; I wanted to comfort her.

"That's great, that's no problem. You found a good fit and that's good, I understand." I wanted her voice to steady and even out, and not hear it falling at the end. I didn't ever want to hear that again. "I'm glad." This last thing I said, stupidly, hoping for relief.

"Thanks, Peter. Yes." She was still unsure. "We found a person, but I enjoyed your audition. I really did."

"Thank you."

We both paused, waiting. I was too shy still and waited for her to find a way out—she was the caller, it was up to her.

The line seemed to fall dead. I heard nothing. I waited and looked at my phone to see the call still open, seconds ticking.

Then, out of that silence: "When did you start playing?"

I was startled but said quickly, "A bit older—early teens."

"How did you start?"

"My grandmother, she—she dropped it off after my grandfather had died. His trumpet."

"Ah. I see that." The line was quiet again for a couple moments. "Do you think you would have played without them giving it to you?"

"Probably not."

"You're not a performer?"

"No. I guess I'm not, really." I thought about the words I had said, I should have told her I was better in a band—but there was no point now. I said, "Maybe I'm not sure what you mean."

"I mean, I guess—is the performance more important than the song? The music itself?"

I knew exactly what she meant. Is the artist more important than the art? "No," I said quickly. "It's not."

"I thought that about you."

It was hard to say what I felt then, except maybe relief, an echo that moved across a long distance and returned to you. My mind emptied.

"When I was seven years old," she said, "my parents bought me a violin. They were strict parents and, you know, the violin is a strict instrument."

I listened, waited.

"I played for a long time but, you know, I was not a performer."

"Yes."

"Anyway, your audition—I liked it because it reminded me of me, I guess."

"I know," I said. "I know exactly. Like trying to talk but you don't know the language. Wanting to listen instead."

"Yes," she said quickly. "I always loved the music. I just wasn't alive in the performance."

"Me neither."

"Honestly, I could never get outside my own head, get lost in it."

"Me too."

"Disappeared in it."

"Exactly. I know."

We had been speaking quickly and stopped at the same time. Again, I waited for her.

Then she sighed. "She's playing tomorrow night. She's remarkable. You can come if you want. You are always welcome at Salottino."

This was goodbye. A small red car pulled slowly through the lot. "Thanks, Lucia." The car started to pull into a space but misjudged it by several feet; it paused and shifted into reverse. The driver's head whipped around, trying to gauge it. "Yes, thank you, I will come by."

She waited, listening. "You're outside?"

"Yeah, I'm at work. Out back." The red car was straightening out to aim into the space.

"Yeah, I'm at my desk behind the kitchen."

The car was getting it, he was going to get in there. I was going to have to end it, she was unsteady in herself. "Thanks for calling, Lucia."

"Thanks, Peter. Come by if you want."

"Yes, I will. Thanks. Goodbye." I pulled the phone away from my ear and ended the call so there wouldn't be anything else. I didn't want to hear words, didn't want to hear silence either.

The front doors of the red car opened. Two men got out, one on either side. They went to the trunk and started unloading boxes. One man had shortish pants and no socks, and in the cold his bare ankles flashed at me.

I went back inside the door and into the kitchen, slipping my phone into my pocket. My heart was breaking. It was falling down in pieces. I went into the bathroom and closed the door and leaned against it, pinning it closed in case anyone else tried to come in, waiting to see if tears would come, already blinking for them. I reached out and flicked the lights off, still leaning on the door. It was a small room with a tight doorframe; the darkness was complete, pressed thick against my face. I listened to my heart beating until it slowed and I knew the tears would not come. In the black room I saw Lucia sitting in that chair with her head in a soft tilt, I saw a droplet on the brass. I was losing something. Confused. I kept breathing as if pushing big sound through my chest. I waited, still pushing and drawing back in, until I felt it. Control. I was okay. I flicked the lights on and stepped out.

Danielle was at the sink, lowering plates. I joined her and started to wash my hands; there was an opportunity to make chit-chat but I was feeling empty of it, so I didn't bother, and she was quiet too—a quiet, undemanding young woman. Something comfortable about those people. It wasn't devastating, but it was a slow and heavy breaking down. Like crumbling. I knew it was the best conversation I had had in months, sober, and I had hardly said anything because I never did. Somewhere behind the disappointment, I felt gratitude, slow-moving and blind. Danielle went out front and I came out to the grill; Stu was moving briskly around it. His eyes flashed when he saw me—busy, stressed—and he gestured to his right, and I knew he wanted me to take over vegetables and salads.

The dinner rush moved quickly, we moved quickly within it, and Stu and I had a good rhythm; I could read him well and adjust, he didn't like to banter when it was busy. But he still wanted to complain. It was his last thing, the only thing he had to take home with him. "Danielle leaves all her plates until they're cold, and tonight we'll get two sent back," he said without looking at me. "If we're lucky. Could be three or four." He glanced up to make sure she wasn't coming to the door. "Marc doesn't care, never says anything."

I slid charred cauliflower onto two plates. Lucia and the violin—that seemed absolutely right.

"The lights keep them warm but not from the inside. It's different."

Elijah came in and slipped past—"Hey Peter," he said—into the back kitchen.

The oven timer dinged and I pulled out two trays of garlic potatoes. I still felt a crumbling inside me but also that slow-moving grace; the brute hangover was gone, letting me move throughout the kitchen, elegant. I felt clean and empty now. There was always a part of me that dreaded getting the job, a small, shameful heart of relief when they say they don't want me. But I was sad too, confused. And knowing that people would ask and I would have to tell them. Being alone with it for the longest possible time was all I had—and it was sand, slipping through. All I had was the dinner rush.

It was close to the end of Stu's shift, and everything was slowing; he brought utensils and extra bowls back to the sink. That's where Elijah was, finishing his shift too, and he washed a few pieces in the sink. It wasn't a formal request—servers didn't have to clean—but he was trying to be a bit nice in his half-hearted, distracted way. When he was done, he went to change in the bathroom. Stu got out the dish gloves and set himself up for a half hour of washing, and, as I was bringing back an empty tray, Elijah returned from the bathroom wearing a long-sleeved shirt and fitted pants, dark blue and black; he was going for his coat hung in the office area.

"Hey, Peter, did they tell you? About the audition?"

"Yeah, she called."

Stu looked up, incredulous.

Elijah smiled, "What'd they say?"

"No—they said no. They had someone else."

"Oh shit, Peter." Elijah's mouth moved downward. "I'm sorry."

"It's okay," I said quickly. "I get used to it."

Stu's face tipped back down in the sink, where he was washing up.

I went out to the grill; Danielle and I would finish up the last hours with Hassan, like last night. It was slow, I pulled out a few extra skewers for late takeout—people on their way home from something else, flushed and tipsy.

"Hey, I'm done." Stu was behind me, removing his apron. "Sorry you didn't get the gig."

"Oh hey, don't worry about it. Actually, it happens a lot." I threw him a small smile over my shoulder before tending to the grill again. "Auditions are hard."

Stu looked hurt anyway, the glimpse I saw of his face. But I didn't look long. I felt cold about it. Cold about him. I wanted to be alone to replay the conversation with Lucia, with her deep and falling voice. I didn't turn around again to say anything else.

Stu said goodnight quietly and left. Shortly after, I started to feel bad for him feeling bad for me. I knew he would think about it and probably mention it again. Sensitive Stu. So dramatically different in so many ways and yet, somewhere near the warm red core, still similar to my sister. But so petty, and sometimes mean—that's how his sensitivity grew into a hard thing. Stu was the one who would feel badly for me, but someone like Elijah, a better person—more benign, anyway—would never think of it again. Those things always confused me, the little ways in which people were backwards, or reversed somehow. I never got used to it.

Hassan was out front in his mixed role, bussing, helping Danielle, and occasionally popping back for something. He would mop at close. It was a demanding role, but it suited him. Hassan was lean and energetic, zipping around the room like a bird. Like Danielle, he didn't socialize much but loved his phone, cradled its gentle blue light in his face whenever he stood in a dark corner. It was a closing shift; I was alone with my thoughts, pushing things around the grill.

I tried to imagine Lucia as a girl, and it was impossible —then I imagined her as a girl with a violin, and I could almost see it. So we were the same, she said. I was embarrassed, grateful for that, a little fragment of honesty that felt like intimacy, but I felt the warmth climbing into my face because it also meant I wasn't good enough, I wasn't the performer she wanted. And I knew what she meant—alive in it. But I knew I would have gotten better as I got comfortable with the band; it always works that way, mostly it was early shakes. But that's how they pick you. There was no time or patience for any other way—I should walk in there filled with blood and heat and set the room on fire. But that was a ludicrous figure for me, lascivious almost, and I was a chaste little boy who wanted to get to know people, get used to the room, before becoming intimate like that; I was a child in that world. And it was not the first time I felt that, a private heartbreak from knowing they did not see me, had not the patience to wait for me, to know me.

Whatever I felt was nothing compared to how I'd feel a month from now. I could reason with fresh disappointment, but in a month I would be lonely. It would be Christmas, I wouldn't have the money from the gig, I would have nothing to wait for.

I wanted a cigarette. Now I felt a late pull after bumming one from Stasi at lunch. But Hassan and Danielle wouldn't have any; nobody smoked anymore. And it would just nudge my hangover awake.

Orders were coming in slower and slower and I had time for small batches of dishes between the dings. The rear building door opened and closed, and I felt a wall of cold air hit my back. Marc was coming in. "Hey, Peter," he said to my back, and went straight to the cooler to put something in.

"Hey, Marc," I said but the cooler was closed and he probably couldn't hear.

He came out. "All good tonight?" he asked as he walked past and into his small office area, with the heavy coats hanging nearby. "Yeah, all good," I said to his receding figure.

He had the black bag and was collecting cash from the back and front. I checked on grill and it was still silent; Danielle followed me back with trays of dishes before going out again. Marc would be here only a minute. I waited for him to cut through the kitchen before leaving—here he was, zipping up the inside pocket on his ancient sheepskin.

"Hey, Marc?"

"Yeah?"

"You wouldn't have a cigarette, would you?"

"Yeah, sure." He rummaged in a side pocket. "I didn't know you smoked. You need a light?"

"No, I can find a lighter in the drawer. Actually, I don't smoke anymore. A craving, I guess."

He gave me a cigarette and wished me a good night and headed out. "Don't start again," he called suddenly, as the door was closing on him, clipping his voice short.

I waited a few minutes for his car to leave from behind the restaurant, but an order gently dinged and I hurried to it, pulling out a skewer and a bun. I'd have five or six minutes now. I went out back before realizing I didn't have a lighter, so I returned quickly and found one in a utensil drawer, then jogged lightly out the back again, then realized I hadn't brought a coat. Fuck the coat, I thought. I'm a smoker again, I don't need a coat. And I lit the cigarette and started shivering almost immediately. It didn't matter; the cigarette was terrible and the whole thing was a mistake.

"Peter, you suck at smoking!" Marc was sitting in his car halfway down the lot, window rolled down, a cloud of his laughing breath moving up in the air. I squinted and held my hand over my eyes—a gesture that made no sense with no sun in the sky—and called back, "Marc, you're still here?"

"Texting. What else." He rolled up his window, got out, and walked over, his boots crunching on remnants of ice and salt. He was pulling out a cigarette too and lit it when he got to me. "Why did you want a smoke?" he asked.

"I'm a bit hungover."

"This just makes it worse, doesn't it?"

"Yeah, it was a mistake, but I don't want to throw it out now."

"You come to work hungover?" he asked. "Not very professional." But he was just batting at me.

"I had soup first. I wasn't that bad."

"I was just joking," he said. "I'm hungover every day."

I didn't know what to say to that. I had taken a pull on the cigarette a minute ago, it was time to take another, and I was waiting an extra beat or two to delay it. Let it burn down a little on its own, it doesn't need me. Marc was a real smoker, puffing happily. He started to pull his phone out of his pocket and I wanted to interrupt him. "So hey. I never asked," I said, and he stopped with the phone for a moment. I took a breath. "What's with the lottery tickets?"

"I'm trying to win a couple mil, obviously." Marc smiled.

"Yeah, but what would you do with it?"

He thought for a minute, looking off into the parking lot. "I'd retire. Move south. Buy a bigger place, nice cars."

I couldn't avoid it any longer, so I took another drag on the cigarette. Awful. And Marc wasn't really answering what I was asking. "I meant, more like, what would you do after that? With all that time."

"I don't know. Not working would be pretty good to start. I'd fill the days with something."

I rubbed my mouth with the back of my cold hand. I was giving up on the cigarette and the conversation and the cold. "I think I've had enough of this," I said, dropping it and rubbing it out. "Forgot how bad it was."

"Told you," Marc said, almost finished his own. "See you tomorrow."

"Saturday—I'm in next on Saturday," I said.

"Saturday, see you then."

I went back inside to the grill, feeling light-headed and disappointed. Kind of up in the blood and low in the mind. I really had to stop talking to people like Marc and Stu.

I don't know what I expected from Marc, but I refused to believe that all the million-dollar dreams of a person would amount only to not working. I've met the non-working already, sometimes they were musicians, with long-suffering spouses carrying them through modest accomplishments, little gigs, a little light on them. That was okay—other people's limping dreams are not mine to mourn. But the non-working are not happy. And the very rich, I imagined, even less so. The self-awareness disappears somehow in that hole; I learned that from my brief gig playing in the steak house. Rich people don't know how unappealing rich people are.

But I didn't have to walk into it every time, with Stu or Marc or anyone else, expecting something nourishing from

a small handful of words—Lucia, I suppose, had opened
me up. And Lucia was not in my life. I lost the audition and
I was going to keep doing this every day. Normally I was
alright with that, but tonight was different.

It started to snow again, and flakes dipped and flew
against the glass; it was heavy, collecting thickly on the
ground. I stood near the back of the small dining room,
tucked near the door, looking out front. Only one table was
left and they were sitting in front of empty plates, talking,
while Danielle cleared another table nearby. Hassan was in
the back, dropping off a tray.

Danielle passed me and went in the door. "I think it will
be an early night," she said brightly, and she was right, the
snow meant early nights, everyone at home, closing heavy
doors, sitting under blankets, looking outside with that
feeling you get from snow. Marc would win the lottery and
fly south and live without snow because it was a nuisance, it
was work, it was shovelling and messy boots—some people
hated winter. Wanted only easy sun.

But enough of this; I flicked off my thoughts because of
course they didn't matter, I was getting bitter, my hangover
had soured and I was down and tired and wanted to go home.
You can't talk to people like Stu or Marc and expect Billy answers; I didn't even know if Billy existed outside of Fifteen.

We washed everything and mopped and closed up. Bye,
guys. I went to the subway with Danielle, but we parted at
the platform, she was northbound. As she turned away, I
remembered she always wore a backpack sagging at the bottom with weight, something I no longer noticed as we left
together. Now that sagging said something to me. I got on
the train and sat down facing the doors, watching them close.
I had tomorrow off. I had booked it in advance because if the

audition had gone well, I knew they would have needed me on Friday evening for my first show. The train started moving through the tunnel. Now I had nothing to do.

LATE NOVEMBER

HEAVY SNOW DRIFTED, languid, through the air. It wasn't falling straight to the ground, it wandered on the moving currents, following people as they walked by, as if it wasn't heavy enough on its own. I had gotten to the restaurant a few minutes early but wasn't expecting Peter for at least fifteen. I had my phone out on the table, face up.

The little restaurant was open for dinner, but the tables and chairs said *lunch*. I knew food service had tight margins, especially in this neighbourhood. I actually liked Peter's restaurant, I had found him that job, but of course he wouldn't want to meet at his work, he was there enough already. This place had large windows along the sidewalk, and I watched people stiffened up in thick coats walking by, careful on the ice. There's something about being inside and warm and looking at people outside and cold—and the reverse, being outside and seeing inside people. We were so far apart; we appreciated things we otherwise would not have seen. I admired those pink cheeks and stiff walks in fat coats, everybody like little children again.

At work, I was still attending the same meetings and looking around at the same circles of turtles. I was disconnected from almost everything and everyone there now. Normally I was *detail-oriented* and *organized* and *responsive* and *reasonably prepared* and *dressed for meetings*, but now I showed up and sat down and let them spin mindlessly, liberated from my attempts to right the ship, get the conversation back on course, finish it, move on—everyone else seemed to prefer two and a half hours of throwing their Rorschach tests on the wall. I had sensed this direction already. I had gone to Isabelle so it wouldn't get too bad, but instead we had made everything worse; somehow we had made everything meaningless.

It was nothing Isabelle had said; frankly, I thought she was going to dispense wisdom and give advice—instead I felt she was an empty vessel simply ready and open. So I poured out. And that was it. The process of me opening and emptying produced some new version that saw everything preceding as tedium, the old self as dead, and whatever lay ahead as vital, blinding, breaking. There was a twisting, downward momentum. Or upward—dizzying. I didn't know how to be at work anymore. I sat in the lot, smoking cigarettes, tapping out emails on my phone.

"You're smoking more," Christopher had said one night.

"Yeah, you smell it, I guess."

"Not that much."

"You should, I'm up to three packs a day now."

To see him grin.

Again I was impatient with Sarah at home. That weary, repetitive parenting—"I know, but." "We have to." "Listen."

"I'm sorry, but."—trying to portion it out, a reliable but disbelieving dosage dispenser of how the world is, our obligations in it, vague reasons why. She occasionally tried to refuse going to school. I had to turn cold and die against it. I had to be firm. I told Christopher it was my fault: I was too structured, I made her feel lost and confused outside our home, I had spent five years working too much, now I was adrift and she was trailing me down. That sensitive child, I knew she knew, she didn't need to be told anything—I would glance up from my phone and she was always watching, her father's eyes wide and still. I loved that little girl. Why did it strike me so heavy in the chest, why did that love weigh so much? It was hard to carry anyone else; for me, it was often everyone else. Mentally I was selfish, but still I had spent my whole life on other people.

"Do you keep in touch often?" In our second-last session, Isabelle had worn a pale green sweater. The Therapy Turtle. Her thick dark hair had been chopped short that time and was now tucked behind her ears. I didn't know whether I should comment on her hair or whether that was an awkward pleasantry in this environment, so I hadn't said anything. Also I didn't think it looked very good.

Isabelle was asking about my father.

"Not so often, just emails sometimes. He lives in Sweden now, that's where she lived. He found a job there too, an American engineering firm."

"You're not close then?"

"Not really." I had said it mildly, but I felt my nostrils flare. How my mother and father had maintained a romantic relationship long enough to result in both Peter and me was unknowable. Maybe he saw something delicate in her, worth protecting. But they were so incongruent, it was absurd. Absurd that I was here. Both of us—persisting long enough to have Peter—showed how good lovers are at lying to each other and themselves. They can keep that up for years. I guess it worked in a way, producing all kinds of incongruent children with rambling patches of each parent, with painful urgencies to know themselves, answer themselves. And here we were, in therapy.

"Do you resent him?"

"No," I had said. I was prepared for that one. "I've thought about it before and I can't resent him. I think it would have been easier on my mother to have a partner, someone to help. She didn't function well on her own. Relied on me mostly, and Peter sometimes." I wasn't looking at Isabelle's face but instead a space on the wall behind her head. "But I don't blame him. We only have this one life, I don't think anyone should give away the whole thing for some obligation. I don't expect that of anybody. I would hate the burden—to be the burden for someone else."

But I never forgave my father for that one summer. His first visit after he moved to Europe, his first visit in two years. He stayed for a week and spent time with Peter and me, taking us to museums and zoos, strange backdrops for bewildered children of a devastating divorce and a disabled mother. Peter was so nervous, he started stumbling over all his words. Almost like a stutter. *Are you stuttering?* Dad would ask. *Slow down when you talk. Slow down, choose your words and speak slowly.* Pointing it out like that, trying to fix him. Asking Mom, *Is he developing a stutter? He struggles with his words.* It made Peter more nervous; when he had to speak, he talked so slowly and carefully, our dad watching carefully, but mostly he avoided talking at all, humiliated in front of the father he hadn't seen in years. It wasn't

even a true stutter. He just stumbled when he got nervous.
Dad took that week with us as an opportunity to fix Peter,
sensing that maybe this sensitive boy was taking after his
mother—maybe he thought this was a helpful piece of parenting he could do. Just pop over from Europe, fix this boy,
pop back. I was still a kid myself and I already knew you
don't do that. You don't pester a frightened kid like that,
you go the other way, you help him feel more comfortable,
and then the stumbling goes away. My father was either
blind or uncaring; absorbing those choices for the first time,
I didn't realize I would see them in my life again and again.

I never told Isabelle about that summer. I forgave my
father for leaving but not for being blind or uncaring when
he occasionally, briefly, came back. If Peter and I were fine-
tuned to tremor and tone, he was all noise and clatter, the
tall father figure with a deep voice and unseeing eyes. But
I was tall like him. And I liked that about myself. I was not
going to be diminutive, forgotten. I was not going to hide.

Peter was coming up along the glass now. I straightened
up, flipped my phone face down.

His face was blotchy from the cold; he wore a lighter coat,
not the type of coat for a day like this, but I imagined his
winter one was bulky and practical. I felt he was trying to
look nice, in the lighter one. That was nice—a small effort
like that. Peter saw me through the window, squinting; he
smiled and waved, still braced against the cold but becoming himself again. He came in and, when the server greeted
him, he pointed at my table.

"Hey, Peter," I said.

"Hey, Stasi." He started pulling open his coat as he sat
down. His face was flushed and cold and shy; we didn't see
each other often, once or twice a year.

"It's cold today," I said. "Time to bring out the winter coat."

"Yeah, I think so."

He looked tired, but his bright eyes were alert.

"Sorry I texted so late last night. Actually, I forgot what time it was and I just remembered we hadn't confirmed lunch."

"It's fine, I was awake." He smiled, his eyes falling toward the table, self-conscious.

"Yeah, you look tired." I looked around the small restaurant. "I don't think I've been here before."

The server came by and asked if we were ready to order, we said we were, we said what we wanted. She was short and joyless and didn't make eye contact during the exchange. She went away.

Peter was looking out the window, as I had been while waiting for him, and there was a pause.

"So how are you? What's going on these days?"

"I had an audition, Monday."

"You're kidding—tell me about it."

"It's a restaurant in the west end, they have a live band two nights a week. A guy I know, a drummer, is in it. Their trumpet player is out for the season, so it's a short-term thing."

"How did the audition go?"

Peter was a bit shy now. "I don't know, really. Sometimes I think I did okay, I did well. Other times I'm not sure." He picked up a cutlery roll and started fiddling with the napkin, folding down a corner. "I don't know how other people see me."

"Did you play with the band? With that drummer you know?"

"No, they couldn't get the band. I was solo."

"Is that harder?"

"Yeah, that's harder."

I started fiddling with my cutlery roll too, mirroring him. We mirrored each other sometimes: I pulled on my ear, he would rub his. Families—you go eight or ten months without seeing them and then you're sitting across from a twin, tied to you with shared moments you never told anyone, never uttered to each other, playing with cutlery or hair or menus in the exact same way. Peter's face looked tired, and there were light red patches on his cheeks, and stubble, but he wore a slim black sweater that looked good on him. I had come from work so I had on a tailored wool blazer.

"At least you didn't forget the trumpet," I said, lightly. I didn't know how to be optimistic about the audition; I knew Peter wanted it, and needed the money. I was nervous for him.

"Hah, yeah," he said, shifting in the chair, looking down at the cutlery.

It was a misfire.

"Well, anyway," I said quickly, "I tried therapy."

Peter looked up.

"Well, I tried it, until recently. I just told her I was taking a break. I went for about a month or so."

"Okay," he said. "Everything alright?"

"Yeah." Now I was really into the cutlery roll. I half unrolled it from the napkin and started straightening the knife and fork. "It was about work. Did I tell you about the VP thing?"

"No. VP, like vice president?"

"Yeah, they opened a new VP role basically right above me and I didn't get it."

"Oh," he said. "I'm sorry. I didn't know anything about it. Who got it?"

"They hired externally. Slapped me in the face. I've been there for fifteen years, helped build that company—they kicked me in the head. Publicly."

"So you went to therapy?"

"Yeah. I got angry and didn't know what else to do. I thought I'd quit. Punish Christopher and Sarah."

Peter nodded. "I know that job means a lot to you." He said it as an offering of understanding from someone who didn't.

I looked out at the street, which was briefly empty. Someone came up along the glass with a small black-and-white dog, its scruffy face tipped up, looking for snow. We both put our cutlery rolls away.

"I guess it is just a job," I said.

Peter looked out the window and saw the dog too. "Dogs don't have jobs," he said.

"Some dogs do, working dogs," I said. "Herders and hunters, all those. They have a purpose bred in them. I guess I'm a working dog."

Peter laughed. "I'm a non-working dog."

The window was empty again. Both of us looked down at our cutlery, but the server came, bringing coffees and waters. Peter and I accepted the cups and saucers noisily and, after she left, spent some time opening little cups of cream, pouring and stirring, stirring and sipping. I asked him if he finally got around to putting himself online—little clips, or anything really—and he gave a wry smile.

"Maybe next year." And that was the end of it. The coffee ritual lasted a few more moments and we were quiet.

"So I stopped." I was musing, alone. "The therapy."

He searched briefly for a moment. "Why?"

The coffee was dark and warm and fired through me gently. I searched around for a few answers, all of them were fine. But the words jumped up and staggered out. "There were some vices in my life, and I wasn't prepared to let go."

"Vices?" Peter asked.

I nodded, but did not say anything else. I sipped the coffee.

"Yeah, I have those," he said. He sipped the coffee, mirroring me. Then we were both looking out the window; it was empty, quiet for a minute.

I wanted to keep it going so I said, "I felt like she was trying to move me toward cutting it out."

"Maybe she thought that's why you came there."

"No, I told her it was about the job."

He nodded. As if he sensed something else but left it there.

The server came back with food. The timing was awkward, as she'd just brought the coffee. The rhythm was off and the service wasn't sophisticated here. We accepted the plates and bowls, rearranged the table. We both had the soup; I also got a side salad—a few hard wedges of tomato and cucumber on pale iceberg—but Peter didn't get anything else. There was a small plate of crackers. We put the bowls in front of us but still worked on the coffee.

"Well, I have vices too." Peter picked it up again. "But I don't think of them that way, as vices. I see them as something else."

"That's good," I said. "I should have told her that."

"What are your vices about?"

"About? What do you mean?"

"I mean," Peter said, taking a moment to find the words, "why do you have them? Do they serve a purpose?"

"A purpose," I repeated. It wasn't clicking with me.

"For me, I guess, my vices are about connection. You know, feeling connected to something. To people."

"Okay." But I gave it up. I didn't know what he was talking about. "I guess I see what you mean."

He could tell I did not. He rubbed the lower half of his face and then his forehead, finally running his hand back through his hair. His face coloured lightly. He was going to try again. "Do you know where the saying 'clarion call' comes from?" he asked.

"Yes, it's a trumpet, right?"

"Yeah—the idea of a call that would bring people together, from afar. Unite them in something, a purpose. I don't feel as if we have that anymore." Peter sipped his coffee. "I feel as if my vices are like that, wanting to disappear into something. But disappearing with others—not alone. A place where we can all feel the same."

"The same? I don't think people are the same." I was brusque with it. "Or if they ever felt that way, it was an illusion—and that time has passed." I bristled against it, I don't know why.

Peter's eyes were out the window again; he said nothing.

I don't know why I stomped it out like that, but it felt familiar, that reflex—Peter would say something earnest or naive and I would stomp it out like flames. Protective maybe? From the disappointments, from the dispossession of innocent people from their innocence.

But I paused and considered—I also wanted to agree with him somehow, reconcile it. "Or maybe that's just me, I never felt the same as other people. I never wanted to."

I stirred the soup and small cubes of vegetables were called up to the surface before sinking below again, disappearing in the reddish broth. No, it was not the same for me as it was for Peter. We were different, whatever his vices were.

He put his coffee aside and started on his soup too, breaking open the crackers first and dropping in the dry, powdery pieces.

My vice was not about connection; it couldn't be. I had so much intimacy already—I had Christopher and Sarah, and it was so much of my life, too much, there were no lines left between us. And so much weight. Mateo was something else, something I had struggled to describe in therapy in a way that felt plain and true, in a way I hadn't rationalized and imposed meaning upon. And that felt right, the struggle to brand him with words. His very name—why not "Matt" like everybody else?—was his separateness from the world; I didn't want to intrude on that. It was a poison, so much knowing, naming of things.

Peter wouldn't understand. He was single but one of those odd creatures who didn't seem lonely, didn't seem driven toward a relationship; it was almost as if he was a little too shy and uncomfortable with it.

"Honestly, I'm not quite sure what my vices mean," I said. "I guess it's an escape. Not that interesting, to be honest."

But Peter had moved on. "Hey," he said, looking down into his bowl, "I wanted to say—I can't pay you back yet."

"Yeah, no problem," I said, "it's nothing." He owed me four hundred dollars from last year. It was a small enough amount that I knew, if he hadn't returned it yet, he was not doing well. He was the type of guy to pay. He brought it up every time I saw him. I wanted to change the topic so I went back to the trumpet. "So do you practise playing much?"

"I did a lot, yeah, for the audition. They picked the songs, I practised them. I came to enjoy it."

"So before the audition, not so much?"

"Not really. I go through phases. I was in a slow phase."

"I get that."

I remembered phases, but from a long time ago. When you have a child, you don't have phases anymore; you react to their development, their milestones, time measured in their way. I probably paid too much attention—in my own distracted way, still watching too carefully. Children know that too; Sarah knew. Christopher was more relaxed than me, willing to let life happen, willing to wait and see—a good balance to me. "I'm going through a smoking phase, I guess," I said.

"That's the vice you were talking about?"

"Hah—no way. It's just a minor chemical."

"People die, though."

"That's true. But it's kind of my style—die of something I did to myself. I'm not a blameless victim."

"I miss smoking." Peter was serious.

"You never smoked much, and not for long. But yeah I guess I missed it too. The work thing, I started again after that."

"I thought I smelled it on you."

"How bad? Out of ten."

"Four. It's not really baked into your clothes and hair yet."

"Thanks."

Heads lowered, we ate our soup. The server came around to look and didn't say anything, retreating again. I could tell she was uninterested in the rhythms of daily life and the strangers within it.

I picked forkfuls of salad from the side plate; I looked at the glass of water and the tiny bubbles clinging to the sides, thinking of Mateo's dark figure leaning against the pale wall. It was a flash in my mind, sending a flare across my body, red and fading.

Outside, a young woman started walking by the diner, buttoned up tightly in a dark wool coat. She seemed warm and happy in there, but unaware of it, and it was a brief comfort to me. Peter was looking down into his soup; his face was still blotchy, and I wondered if he was drinking, he looked dehydrated.

We finished lunch and I paid. We stood at the table, pulling on our coats. "Back to work for me," I said.

"Yeah, I have a closing shift tonight. But I'll go home first to change."

"I could drop you off at your place?"

"Great."

I turned to the back of the small restaurant. "Thank you," I called out to the server across the room; she looked up as we turned and headed for the door, her face blank. "Ready for the cold?" I asked Peter.

"Never, really," he said. I pulled open the door of the restaurant, and the stinging air rushed our faces and hands. We tucked our heads down as we headed to my car.

It had stopped snowing, but there was a soft white surface on everything around us. But it was a relief to get inside the car and fire up the engine, knowing warm air was coming and would hold us in tight. It was so pleasing to me and yet I knew some people had no winters. Coming in from the cold and becoming warm wasn't the same as the reverse—coming in from the heat into an air-conditioned, artificial coolness—a brisk relief. This was something specific, a thick, tight comfort. And yet some people had no winters, where was that feeling for them? Or did they not have that anywhere? The feeling was so singular and right to me, I couldn't imagine entire lives without it—hot climates never knowing the solace of warmth.

I wanted a cigarette; I pulled a pack from the compartment in front of Peter. "You want one?"

"Sure, okay," he said.

We lit up and opened the windows a few inches as I pulled out of the lot and waited for a lane to open.

"God, Stasi, this is awful."

I snorted. "Poor baby. What's it been, a couple of years?"

"Eight, I think. Also you smoke terrible cigarettes. They taste like death."

"Exactly," I said. "It's appropriate. You get used to them; you have to push through the first five or six and then you're hooked again so you ignore the taste."

Peter flicked the lit cigarette out the car window and closed it. "No thanks."

"Poor baby Peter," I said. "And his pretty little throat."

"That's right," he said.

"Can't ruin it for the gig."

"Maybe."

"When do you find out, by the way?"

"Today."

"Today?"

"Yeah, she said Thursday. She'll call me at some point." He pulled out his phone and looked at it before tucking it back into his pocket.

"Shit, Peter." I opened the window a few inches further and threw out my cigarette. "Can't poison you in here."

"Hey, you didn't have to do that," he said.

"It's okay, I don't care." I checked a passing street sign to orient myself. "It's killing me anyway."

"Grandpa," he said.

"Yeah, right. Grandpa."

"But his lungs were wrecked from before, I guess."

"That's true."

I looked at the time. "So. We have about fifteen minutes in the car." I changed lanes, restless. "What do you want to talk about?"

"I don't know." His head turned slightly, looking out the window. "What do you want to talk about?"

"Well, the therapist." I waited a moment. "She seemed disturbed when I told her about Mom dying—I said I didn't have time to grieve. I pushed it to the side." Peter didn't say anything. "Work was busy, as always."

"So the therapist didn't like that?"

"Well, she didn't say anything, but I could tell it was a problem. Her face changed."

"So it bothers you?"

"I guess I wanted to know—did you take time to grieve? I mean, I don't exactly know what that means. Like spending time at her grave, talking to the stone? Journalling?"

"Yeah, I don't know what it means either," he said.

"So did you grieve?"

"Yeah, I think I did." But as the words were out, he set to correct them. "But people grieve differently—and you know, I think—I always thought it affected you more. Like you were closer. You took care of her when we were at home."

"Yeah, I was oldest."

"Yeah." The car was quiet. Peter kept his face toward the window.

"So how do you know when you've grieved and it's over?"

"I don't know. Did you ask the therapist?"

"No."

Peter's hands were in his lap and he opened them, palms up, looking into them. "And you stopped going?"

"Well, I told her I was taking a break." We stopped at a red. "But yeah, I'm not going back, I don't think. Not now. I think some processes started and I want to be alone with it. I told her the HSP thing and I think I need to be alone to let everything land."

"Okay," he said.

We were quiet again, waiting at a light. My fingers drummed the wheel, fidgeting, but I noticed and let my hands slip off.

"I went to a visitation for this girl," I said, "this poor young girl in the neighbourhood, a car accident. And I felt anxious there. Light-headed, spinning, I had to leave. And with Mom's funeral before that, I don't remember any of it—just this numb thing."

"Well, you had to organize the whole thing. I couldn't—I didn't know what to do."

"Yeah," I said.

I didn't know what I was asking for, so I let it go.

Traffic let up and we were moving again. The shops were getting smaller, the big chains were disappearing, store signs were colourful and crowded. We were getting closer to his neighbourhood.

"If it helps—I don't know if it helps—" Peter started to say. "With grieving I mean." He paused to find it. "You know, I don't think she was unhappy."

"Mom?"

"Yeah," he said. "I mean—I don't think she was unhappy."

"She barely left the house. She was terrified of everything."

"She was scared of people," he said. "Of embarrassment, judgment. And she was right—people judge."

"She didn't have any kind of life."

"Yeah, but—I mean—I don't think she was actually unhappy." He was trying to get me to hear it. "I don't think she wanted a kind of life like other people do. I think she was happy where she was—safe. At home."

I understood what he was trying to say. "So her death—so her life and death—is less sad, then?"

"I don't know," he said. "Sad is another judgment I guess. I just mean—I don't think she was unhappy. I never thought of her like that. Some people have normal lives and they are unhappy anyway. I don't think she was."

"Yeah, I don't know. I always thought the whole thing was fucking depressing."

"Because you had to deal with it. You were grown up at ten."

The acknowledgment, coming from him, caught me dead centre. Like blame and forgiveness arriving at once— heavy and breathless. It was heavier than ten sessions in therapy. "Sometimes I don't remember a childhood at all."

His face was turned to the window. "Yeah," he said. "I get that."

I took a full breath. Exhaled, moving gently with traffic. A weight, somewhere, had shifted.

We got to Peter's place. That was the end of it; he got out of the car. But he didn't close the door right away, he dipped his head down and said, "How about us?"

For a second I thought he was still talking about Mom.

"You said you never felt the same as anyone else," he continued. "What about us? Did you ever feel we were the same?"

"No, no," I said quickly, remembering his talk from lunch. Then I started grinning. "No way—we're opposites."

He grinned back. But his eyes reddened in the cold.

I told him to text me later about the gig, if he wanted. He said sure—but I knew if I didn't hear from him it was because he didn't get it. Bye, Peter. Bye, Stasi. See you maybe at Christmas? Sure, maybe. And Peter closed the door and walked away from the car. I had invited him over last Christmas after our family had reduced to just us, with Dad thriving over in Europe, but he didn't end up coming for the dinner; he came a few days later for a little visit, holding a little drugstore box of chocolates. I thought he felt uncomfortable joining me and Christopher and Sarah, as if it was an intrusion. It wouldn't have been. But I knew in his position I would have felt the same.

I watched him, hands in pockets, face tipped down, walking along the street toward his apartment. "Bye, Peter," I said aloud, alone in the car. I forgot about him sometimes, but whenever he was leaving, I missed him. A small and swift pain.

I got out another cigarette out and opened the window. It was a quarter after one and my phone was vibrating occasionally, collecting work emails. Maybe a text from Christopher. I suddenly remembered my other phone—I hadn't checked it that morning. It was just a random Thursday, probably nothing, but I had a minute while I smoked so I went deep into my bag.

The phone started up slowly. Messages loaded. I couldn't believe how many, scrolling up and down. My heart stirred painfully in my chest, alarmed. He did not talk like this. Something was happening.

Stasi stasi

I have been drinking

Nothing special, Eduardo from work but he went home and I stayed at the bar

And I have been thinking

I rested the phone on my thigh, face down, for a moment, putting my head back. Fuck. They were from late last night.

He was leaving.

I turned the phone face up again.

You did not tell me about your mother

Her dying

I don't know why ?

Are we really so cold .. ?

Tonight there is good music playing at this bar

At least 4 or 5 songs from when I was young
It feels good when drinking to hear old songs
This is like a long letter I am writing someone
I don't write letters
Anyway
You are at home in bed
With Christopher
I don't even like his name, it doesn't suit you
Anyway I won't be driving home I've gone too far
It was good to hear those songs again
You should have been here

He didn't talk or message like this; he was drunk. I went back through them again and looked at the time—a few came quickly, a couple were spaced by a half hour or more. He was struggling with something, but I didn't know what he was saying, whether the man was talking through the whisky or the whisky through the man. It sounded lonely. The car felt small around me. I looked out the windshield at the small, snowy street. My head fell back into the headrest and I tapped my cigarette out the window.

What did he want? Mentioning my mother—offering sympathy? Intimacy? The comment about Christopher's name—a jealous stab? Was he trying to break free in a backwards way—a provocation, a confrontation, a push to see which way I would fall? He was kicking through a wall of smoke, he was drunk and a little sad. Or was it a game? One day he pulls me closer, the next he pushes me away; he feels me twist in the confusion, he sees his power. Maybe he didn't want a woman at all, he wanted that power—secretly inside himself, unknown to himself. The whisky was making him honest, not in words but intention; ignore the words but watch where they ask you to go.

If I saw Isabelle again, I would tell her about me. I would tell her what I hadn't been able to tell Christopher or anyone else. I had two hearts. People with one heart don't get it, and they want you to have one heart like them—but you don't. They want you to close one and keep the other and have that only, because it's wrong to be the other way—selfish. And I could see that. I told myself that too. And I knew the lying was like death, creeping under the surface until the ground split and it came up hot, obliterating everything else, but it was also the truth, unflinching, inevitable, final. If you have two hearts, you will be pained or cause pain, likely both, a lot of each, yet nothing saves you, nothing cures that second heart, nothing kills it. Guilt and shame glance off at soft angles, inert. The meaningless trivialities of single-hearted people. In fact, it grows stronger as you get older; it grips you at the throat until your eyes burn hollow. It reminds you when you try to live without. And if my family found out, it wouldn't be the devastation of the lying, it would be that I was now finally telling the truth, and they finally knew who I was— and who I was was wrong.

What Mateo really wanted I couldn't know; when you sleep with a stranger over and over, you wake up alone in a room of mirrors. He was a cipher. He was drunk last night and regretting everything today.

I couldn't write anything back.

Fuck.

The messages were already more than twelve hours old. I knew he would be waiting today, checking his phone. It was already after lunch; he would give up looking at his phone, but then he would be back again within the hour, the ache and hope met with a fresh sting, nothing, that free fall of disappointment. I remembered the years of checking my phone to see if anybody loved me. Just any kind of notification at all.

Mateo couldn't understand what he was doing. He didn't want intimacy. I knew he had two hearts, but he was naive if he was trying to merge them, thinking he could have only one and be the same—intimacy was the end game. It would domesticate a woman and begin the slow erosion, looking out instead of in, that would turn him restless within a few months, his second heart grasping at nothing. He was older than me, he had done this before—and still he didn't know? Was that possible? That stupidity was costly at our age, a shameful stumble.

But I suspected worse: he was drunk and trying to run, and too cowardly to do it himself. He fired a shot and hoped for obliteration in return.

The circular truth of it was most shameful of all, because I had done this first; I had stumbled early and he had been so cold, unthinking, when I had clawed for him with some kind of blank weariness—after a long, slow day and a lot of wine. With complete coldness he had brushed me aside, and while putting myself back together, I kept fucking him. And I saw myself for what I was, I had tested him on purpose, the wine making me sloppy and honest. Two-hearted but unknown to myself, I had been trying to run.

The phone came alive suddenly in my hand.

Stasi I am sorry

I was drinking too much last night

I waited, looking at the phone. It was silent again in my hand.

A few minutes later it lit up again.

How are you today

He was bruised.

I sent a heart, the smaller one, and turned off the phone. I would not say anything until tomorrow, and I knew that would hurt him.

You had to learn how to do this, how to hurt each other in small ways; you had to see tenderness for the threat it was and leave little scars to keep the surface strong. I had gone first, now it was his turn. I put the phone at the bottom of my bag, finding the gap in the lining.

I finished my cigarette. I felt sad.

Mateo was lost and I was supposed to say something true to him. I never knew how I always ended up here, responsible for someone else.

The car was idling, warm; I had to get back to work. I thought briefly of Peter in his apartment now. Poor Peter, with no one. Or lucky perhaps, escaping intimate loneliness for solitary loneliness—lighter, cleaner, in a way. I looked again out the windshield expecting someone to be walking by who made me feel a certain way, like things were right again. An older couple maybe. A father with his young child, or a mother. But there was nothing. Only shapes without any faces within them and I couldn't see anything properly, something inside of me was staggering out. Mateo didn't know who he was, did not see the truth, and someone was going to have to tell him. It seemed it was supposed to be me. I put the car in drive and checked for traffic. I pulled out in a tight U and joined the lane in the opposite direction. The lane was open and, with gathering resolve, I pressed the pedal, surging slowly and then fast. I knew myself anyway. The light ahead was still green and people on the sidewalks were starting to blur. One thing I knew—I could never be like them.

FRIDAY

THERE WAS a small window in my bedroom and a square of yellow light was broken against the top of the dresser and the wall behind it. When I woke, my eyes opened on it. The light was hard and bright, it would be cold outside; I rolled onto my back and looked up at the ceiling. Should I get up, or were there any dreams left? There was something warm in my chest and I was trying to hold onto it, look at it, but it was quietly leaving. I folded my arms behind my head. I had nowhere to be today. A black shadow flickered across the yellow square on the wall—a bird—I only just caught it from the corner of my eye. Maybe I would go for a walk, in the cold.

I ignored the text from Stasi and showered. If I was slow to respond she would already know and it would give her time to accept it—otherwise she would get fired up, always reacting for everyone, a big guard dog on a long chain. I phrased my response under the hot water. I got dressed and slipped on shoes and jogged downstairs to Ibrahim's for a tar-black coffee, slowly carrying it back up between my hands, already cold from the snapping air outside. I brought it to the sofa and sat down, looking out the window. A cold day would feel good, it always did—a sharp discomfort, weathering it, a grateful return home. I finished the coffee and picked up my phone.

No I didn't but it's okay. They are hard to get
I am disappointed but maybe not surprised
Then,
I can still pay you back later, maybe in a couple months

I didn't want to eat or wait for her reply so I put on my boots and heavy coat and hat. My gloves were already in the pockets. Standing there in full winter suit, I packed a quick pipe and took a long haul, fragrant smoke drifting across the room and into the sunlight. As I left, I heard a soft sound from my phone on the coffee table. I closed the door and pulled the bolt through the lock. I liked leaving my phone sometimes—unnerving at first, but fleeting, then a kind of clean emptiness.

High above the street, the sky was brittle blue and lonely for clouds. I started walking west out of habit, where the park was.

With the audition done and lost, I didn't know what to think about; it had been the central thing for a couple of weeks and now it was over, another disappointment to scatter as dust. A light coating on everything. There was enough of that already, so it was not a new thing, only a heavy thing, something that collected weight as the years went by. My mind was empty now, looking for something gentle. After the pipe, I was high and searching.

I got to the park and started along the path, passing benches full of people, set into the grass. All the benches had showed up one year, out of nowhere. There had been no benches before. This mysterious and quiet public formation changed the entire park. The park was almost always full now because so many people stopped and sat, suspended between where they'd come from and where they were going, even in the cold, like picture frames with little snapshots along the way. Benches—I bet Billy could talk about that for a while. It was something he had probably thought about, and he must have been a bench guy, absolutely one to sit down. They show up a lot in movies—an important scene between two characters, something is changing, something is being revealed; there they are in a leafy park, sitting on benches. Without them, my walk would have been mostly alone. I would mention it to Billy and, drunk in a loud basement, we would see something in it.

I found an empty bench and sat down. It was hard to ignore the cold because I hadn't had any breakfast, only the one coffee, and it wasn't a very large one. I crossed my arms, pressing all the heat down. Stasi had been in therapy. Perhaps I could have thought of that as inevitable, but I also knew her well enough to know she would demand nothing for herself as she fought for everything else. But then she had decided to stop therapy—some kind of blanking in her. I thought maybe she was unsure of herself and how far she wanted to go. What did Stasi want? If you want to think about how well you know someone, answer that question about them—what do they want?—and if you have an interesting answer, one that is true, you probably know that person very well.

What did Stasi want? It was a good question. I think she wanted people to listen to her, which, perhaps, was odd, because I think she had spoken her mind strongly from a very early age. Maybe she still felt ignored in some other way, maybe she thought she was heard but not understood. In that sense, I thought this whole thing about the VP job was actually a very good example—she wanted to be the boss and really do her work her way, and watch those numbers climb; she loved success almost as much as anything. She liked that she could change something and control it with her efforts alone. All of that was very Stasi. Our parents actually named her Anastasia and she never used it, but if you say it aloud, you get an idea of how complicated she is. Her short little nickname was a trick.

OK, so if Stasi wanted everyone to listen to her, what would she say? I didn't know that part. She was a solitary person by nature, no matter who was in her life; I could only imagine an empty howl. Seeking an echo maybe.

I knew what Billy wanted. He told me many times in different combinations and usually drunk, over loud music. "I want people to care! To care! To care! To care until it breaks their hearts!" That would be carved on Billy's gravestone at the end of his life, it was his little religion; he was obsessed with the idea that people did not care enough. About anything. That part—care about what?—was vague. But he knew the big part was true.

I crossed my legs and I was a bit warmer. Slowly I was closing up my body, crossed arms, crossed legs, but these were the last limbs available to wrap together. There was a couple on the bench to my right, leaning into each other, both with steaming coffee cups. This was a crucial error, that I did not bring something warm for my hands and throat. I was paying for it.

I remembered Horse from all those years ago, all he had said to me—me, a stranger taking his found trumpet away. He just talked and talked. He'd been called to a war and then sent home, brushing against a great tragedy with all the other men, luck giving him life and sending him back, still fully connected to everything. He had been called to something so big it may have cost him his life. And he came back.

I never had that. I never had anywhere to go—or people to go with. I wondered what that felt like, one body moving as a great mass of others, whether you felt brave, or less alone. Whether it felt important. I didn't have that in my life, and it was unclear what exactly that meant because I was not lonely for one person. I was alright when I was alone in that way. No—it was something tall and wide. I couldn't quite make it out. But it was almost as if I was lonely for this idea—not religion, not war, not with that damage. But called to something and everybody shows up. An immaculate connection. The idea comforted me from far away, a home I never knew myself.

I would start thinking about Lucia soon, and the audition, but I wasn't ready for that yet. I was too cold. And still stoned. Maybe with some core heat I could bring it up and parse it over, but not now, and not here, numbing on a bench.

I got up and walked through the rest of the park. The path curved around clusters of trees, most of them bare, with some old blue spruces holding out their long, shaggy arms. I walked by people with dogs, couples, singles, one family with a tiny proud dog walking way out front. People on benches got up and started walking too, probably cold like me. It was hard to linger, but I liked seeing so many people about. The park path wound around, but I moved briskly and soon I was at the end of it, on another sidewalk, and I turned back home. I would get another coffee from downstairs before making some breakfast. I didn't know what to do with the rest of the day, but there was a good chance I'd end up smoking it away, listening to records, making food, ignoring the case on the shelf, ignoring what I felt in my chest and stomach. What else to do with a day I had put aside for a gig I wouldn't get?

I was walking along some row houses on the empty side-walk when one of the doors opened on one of the homes and a woman ran out; she was holding a jar and wearing an apron. Her feet were in red house slippers. I was arrested by the sight of her running out into the cold air and I stopped walking a brief moment before I noticed, with confusion and eventually alarm, she was running toward me.

"Hey, hi," she said, bright and breathless. She seemed a bit older than me, there was a flush high on her cheeks.

I had stopped on the sidewalk, caught in surprise, and couldn't summon any words right away. She jumped in again quickly.

"I can't open this." She held out the jar to me, her eyes flashing in triumph with her little ploy. "I have two kids at home. I thought, I'll run out and see who's on the street. Or ask a neighbour. But I saw you first."

"Oh, sure," I said. I took the jar from her but still had my gloves on, so I pulled them off and tucked them into my pockets one at a time. It was strained tomatoes. The jar was slightly warm from inside the house and, presumably, her attempts to pull it open. I gripped the glass jar with one hand and the lid with the other and gave it a hard, brutal twist—it held completely tight. I looked at the jar, incredulous. "Serious?"

"Right?" she laughed. "I can do jars usually. I'm not that weak."

I turned the jar over to hit the bottom.

"I did that too. A couple of times."

I whacked the bottom again anyway before turning it over and giving another hard, wrenching twist. Nothing. No give at all. "This is wrong," I said, looking at the jar in my hands.

She seemed pleased it wasn't easy for me either. "And I hit the lid too."

"Yeah, I was going to ask."

We both stood there looking at the jar in my hands. "You know," I said, "some garlic, cream, butter, some grated cheese if you have it, black pepper—it's a good sauce. Bone broth, mushrooms, if you have them."

"We're giving up?" she asked, incredulous. "My kids won't eat that."

"No, no," I said, "not giving up. One more, let me try." And I bent slightly and wedged the jar between my knees, holding it with one hand and gripping the lid again with the other. Somehow, that position, how my arms were pointing down—suddenly the lid gave the merest breath of movement. I twisted hard again and it slid free. "There it is." Now it was easy; I gently spun the lid around in relief. I handed the jar to her.

"Oh thank god," she said. She looked at it in her hands, and I noticed they were bare and already pink with cold; she had brought no coat or gloves with her as she dashed outside. "Thank you," she said, smiling.

I felt shy in front of her smile so I didn't quite make eye contact but my voice was bright and friendly. "Yeah, no problem at all." And I was genuinely satisfied the jar had come open in my hands, a pleasure and a relief. My hands tingled softly.

She turned to go back in the house, and I started walking again.

I felt a little bit buzzy. The sidewalk was mostly empty but every couple of minutes I would pass someone: first a nondescript woman with grocery bags, then a nondescript man in snow boots. Eventually I started to see better: two teenagers, one tall and mouthy, the other rounder and shy, you could tell they would be friends for a long time. A curly-haired father walked by with his curly-haired daughter, she was wheeling a bike and just old enough to keep up with him. I gave them a little extra space to get by. It was such a pretty thing, a girl with a bike in the winter cold. That's how I would describe it to Billy, that it was a pretty thing to run out and ask a stranger for help on something so small. It took a bit of faith. And Billy would agree with that.

I went back into Ibrahim's for coffee. "Another one?" the guy said. It was one of the younger men that worked there, ridiculously lanky and tall, a broom with arms.

"Yeah, it's cold out," I said. "And I have the day off." The significance of that didn't really seem to fit, but I guess I was telling him.

"Okay," he said. His uniform was a white shirt and white apron, still very clean, impressive, especially at waist-level for the apron. The small takeout place was also very white on the inside. He brought me a short, lidded cup.

"Thanks," I said. The cup was small in my gloved hands but I knew, gratefully, how bitter and black the brew was inside.

"No problem," he said, now actually picking up a broom and pushing it around.

I went upstairs to my place, struggling a bit with my key and the door handle as I held the coffee. It was good to walk into the warm, small place. I took off my boots, hung up my coat and hat, and brought the cup to the sofa. Something felt lighter in me. But I saw my phone on the table. And Stasi was waiting. Phones were such disappointments; either they had nothing in them and you felt bad about that, or they had messages and now you had work to do, responding. I picked it up, there was her response.

Fuckers

They should have picked you

Oh well their loss

I don't care about the money Peter

Don't worry about it

A little more casual than I was used to, but I preferred Stasi this way, rather than something meek—*I'm sorry you didn't get it, keep getting out there, keep trying, you'll get the next one*—or some other combination of empty phrases. I read over her messages again; they didn't even need a response. So she was releasing me from that obligation. I knew what Stasi would do next: she would search and read up about the restaurant and find a bad review or other diminishing information; she would sleep better having read that. Then the next time she saw me, she would casually drop it in—*Oh did you know that Salottino place got rats one summer?*—and she would be satisfied, shots fired, enemy dropping to the ground. She would make all this effort thinking it was for my sake, but I did not need this, I did not need to make enemies.

I put the phone back down and had the coffee, thinking.

I didn't even remember what the woman had looked like. It was too surprising, I thought I was watching something else happening but then I was part of it, I was involved, this stranger running out was indeed running up to me. Now that I was alone with my coffee, and warm again inside, I wanted to recall it once more, this innocent thing. I think she had brown hair down to her shoulders and an animated face. That's about all I remembered.

I picked up my phone and searched for "Lucia" and "Salottino." I had never gotten her last name. I thought maybe she had done an interview at some point about the restaurant, or showed up in a review—I thought she'd be somewhere. I scrolled for a while, but there was nothing; I threw the phone back on the table.

What now? Breakfast. And the day? Maybe I would get some food in the evening. I looked around the four corners of the room. I could play a little bit, it was the kind of thing that felt good on a cold day; I went up to the case, looking at it, but the mood suddenly failed me. So I went to the kitchen instead to make something to eat.

The hours passed slowly, like a spider crossing the ceiling. I took occasional puffs on the pipe throughout. I spent a good deal of the afternoon watching a series of shortish documentaries about multi-generational, family-owned shops from around the world. I kind of forgot what I was doing for about half of a documentary but a new one would follow right after, so I kept going. The families all seemed nice, but the production was slick and flashy, annoying at times, and made me think of a hyped-up camera crew and editing team, trampling over their little stories. I didn't know anything about documentaries, but I knew some musicians like that—trampling.

When the series ended, I felt stiff and sluggish on the sofa. I should have taken another walk to get some food, takeout from somewhere small. Ibrahim's had great plates actually, but I had already been there twice today, I didn't want them to feel sorry for me. Outside the window, it was dark.

I started getting my boots on, thinking of the cold, which would be even more bitter now. And suddenly it hit me. Like two great bolts to the chest. It hit me—it would be a cold, dark winter and I had nowhere to go.

I stopped with the boots for a moment and let the disappointment flood me with a brief and wild despair. Lucia said we were alike, but they had found someone else. And who? Someone easy and confident, lascivious, a born performer? How could Lucia choose that? I had been avoiding it all day, but it was waiting for me, kicking me in the chest right when I was putting on my boots. They had found someone else. I was alone for the winter. Another winter.

Well. I deserved a drink. It was going to be another year that passed with nothing; I had so many now behind me. I knew how to do this—disappointment and letting time pass. But I had earned a drink. I had no money, but I had earned a drink. The woman with the jar who came out running; her brazenly small request, her radical little act, breaking down walls between strangers like that—didn't even remember her coat. It had to be a humble thing like that to tell me which way to go. I was getting a drink.

I went to my closet and pulled on black pants, a grey collared shirt, and a glossy black silk tie. Black socks. I got my shoes from the closet. I pulled out my lighter wool coat that was cut nicely against my chest, not as warm but twice as snug. No hat. I was going to be cold but sharp as a dagger, dangerous almost, distanced from everybody else. But I was never as brave as all that; I took two quick shots of Scotch, the lone bottle in my cabinet.

I did not go toward the subway but instead kept along the street where I knew there was a joint that sold a stick of heavily buttered garlic bread for less than two dollars.

Just a shortish stick wrapped in foil; normally it was only a side order with a takeout meal, but they would sell it to you if you were off the street and had a certain look—hungry and alone, I guess—and they could tell you needed a cheap fill before going out. I always passed the test. "Can I get the garlic bread?" and the man would look at me and punch it in—"Sure, no problem"—and then nod to the next customer. It was good of him. I waited for the foil-wrapped stick and headed back into the cold, opening the tip and biting into the hot bread and salty, buttery, garlicky filling. I walked along the street eating quickly, in large sideways-tearing bites, and got on the subway when I was finished.

Salottino's door seemed something from a long time ago, dreamlike. But I felt good again. The Scotch and the bread had put an arm around me, like a friend. I felt brave enough to go inside and, through the glass, I could see a lot of backs facing out—it was crowded.

The humid warmth hit me as I opened the door. It was noisy. It was almost immediately overwhelming; clusters of people by the door waited to be seated, but the place wasn't full yet. The line was moving briskly as the host came up and swept them away in twos or threes. There was momentum already. I unbuttoned my coat and smoothed my cold hair back with my hand; my ears burned as the aching cold left them. I had forgotten Salottino was mostly red on the inside. It made the place flushed and hot and exciting, coming in from the blue-black night.

"Just me," I said to the host when I got up to the stand. "No reservation, but Lucia invited me." The host was floppy-haired and immaculately dressed, unsmiling, seeming in her fifties or sixties.

I was skirted along some larger tables and out to a tiny circle near the back, somewhat tucked behind a mirror-covered column. But I could still see the stage. Plates of blue glass glimmered almost purple in the soft red glow of the room. I felt high, almost, seeing it again. Seeing it without the threat of the audition, it was a body rush—I had been standing there?—and as my server came near, I said, "Rye and soda," and with a nod he turned around before reaching me and went back to the bar. It was busy, tables were full all around me, I thought he would appreciate that from a single guy at a small table—no need to fuss the service. People were dressed well, polished, in dark colours, as if we were all participating in something. Maybe the same thing. Phones popped up in the air every so often.

My server came by with the drink; it was fast, they were serious here. He left a short menu, but I knew I couldn't afford anything, so I looked all around the room and lingered on groups of friends, families and couples. Friends were having the most fun, and were at the largest tables; families and couples were more interesting. In a family almost each person was different, the animated and the bored and everything in between; in couples there was more boredom and eyes around the room. But sometimes you saw a new couple with fire in their eyes and it made you feel something. It was dangerous, alive, and it was bittersweet, as if the ending was always buried there in the beginning.

My first drink was gone. The server was circulating and our eyes met for another. There was soft piano in the background, plain and pleasing, and I went slower with the second drink, sipping briefly and spending longer stretches not sipping.

Since Stasi had brought it up, me forgetting that trumpet so long ago, Horse kept surfacing in my mind. He had been so lonely and by now he would be dead. Lonely people talk a lot to strangers—Billy was like that—and old people were often lonely. Nobody saw them, young people saw only each other, middle-aged people were wearily lost in their own lives. A war veteran must be the loneliest of them all. Sitting in parks, waiting in grocery lines, circling quiet suburbs, resuming ordinary and serene lives, the roar still in their ears.

The stories about trumpets kept finding me—I never sought them out but they surfaced, often around this time of year, around veterans and remembrance services. The captain who played the trumpet over the apple orchards of Normandy when they knew one German sniper remained hiding under the cover of night. Still, he played. He played the German love song, "Lili Marlene." And by morning they had a German prisoner on the beach, a boy of nineteen, asking who played the trumpet last night. And the young sniper wept. He missed his girl, his family; he could not fire, he was done. He shook the captain's hand.

A boy of nineteen, a child, sent into war. As a sniper. Alone.

I once worked a season with a dishwasher who was living in the city for the summer—he was from PEI, several generations deep. He was directly descended from one of the farmers who, in the 1800s, refused to pay rent to landlords in Britain, and when the sheriffs came, neighbours blew tin trumpets across the countryside. Dozens would arrive, surrounding the farmers and preventing their arrest. When troops were called in—most of whom were actually Irish—they sided with the farmers. The dishwasher told me all this with enormous energy, his red arms deep in the soapy water, because I had mentioned I played the trumpet.

The tin instrument was still in their living room, all these generations later.

My generation had nothing like that. Instead we had some kind of loneliness, growing up in empty spaces and then everything becoming so connected and so crowded out there. Disappearing you. It was vague and hard to describe and you knew it meant nothing to anyone else, your private aloneness. Alone on a dark beach, no rifle, no song, no war, no enemy, and no friend, nowhere to surrender, no call to make, none that would come.

My second drink was gone, even though I had tried to go slowly. I always drank too fast and that was the best way for a night to go south. For me to go on and on about the loneliness as I sat alone in a public place, drinking. We knew the best drugs already. Wanted children, lives of humility and connection. Stop talking about yourself, stop thinking about yourself, get lost in a crowd, get lost and don't even tell anybody about it. Tell absolutely no one. For whatever reason, so much less lonely that way.

The server came by, my reliable friend, my heart surged a little to see him. If you have a good server, it's easy to fall in love with them. And two down, I was feeling bold. I wanted to do something like the woman who ran out of the house toward me, forgetting her coat. So when my server came, a wild impulse darted out of me and I said, "Lucia is buying my next round."

He gave a smile, neat, and went off again.

The band was showing up now: a man in a white shirt and black pants climbed onto the stage and opened a saxophone case. Then there was Boris, climbing up and getting to the drums at the back; he looked well-built in his white shirt, his good drummer's arms, but the overhead blue lights catching on his rough, pockmarked face. He always looked a lot older than he actually was. A woman came up and moved behind the keyboard, then the bassist followed. All of them wore the black pants and the white shirts, gleaming in blue under the cool lights and sapphire-glittering stage.

And she was last, tallish and striding. Her white shirt was cuffed back to the elbows, and the shock of dark, elaborate sleeve tattoos stopped abruptly at her wrists. She opened a case and pulled out a silver trumpet, turning around to face the room. Her hair was another shock, platinum and shaved on the sides, leaving a long band of hair down the middle of her head and down her back. With her white shirt and silver instrument and near-white hair, her dark forearms were dramatic, like war paint.

Her face was cold.

If it was me up there, on a first night, I'd certainly be trying for the stone-cold face—but I would not be succeeding.

My server came back and, with an appraising tip of his head, set my drink down in front of me. "Lucia says hello," he said before leaving the table. Behind him, at the bar, I saw her silhouette retreating into the back kitchen, her hair still plainly parted down the middle, tied back.

The band was winding up, then seemed to pause. Boris counted them in; everything dropped into place with the opening few keys. I scanned for it, couldn't place it, until the sax took the vocal, a hard growl smoothing out into pure tone, adding a little vibrato. "Cry Me a River."

Julie London—a teenager singing in LA nightclubs in the forties. As the world disappeared into war, this young woman, this child, singing in dark clubs.

The trumpeter stood there holding the instrument loose at her side. I studied her face in the blue light, something of the child in her wide cheeks and dainty nose, despite the war-paint arms and band of hair. The sax was gorgeous, and the room hushed into its smoky sound; I saw Boris behind him moving gently with his head lowered. I drained my drink almost completely.

It was a mistake to come here. I had wanted this so badly and couldn't even find the heart to be angry, only heartbroken, endlessly heartbroken. It would be easier to be angry. I was going to get drunk here and I didn't even have the money for it. And then, at the end, the sax faded away and she brought the instrument up to her mouth to join his last notes; she ended the song high and bright—was that a ninth?—as clean as a blade, but soft, as if from a distance, her bell tipped back from the mic. Her face unchanged, as if she had done nothing. It was bold to end the song like that—whose arrangement?

I finished the drink with failing bravado, alone at my table, collapsing on the inside.

Light patters of applause rippled around the room.

With the first song over, most of the tables resumed their night, talking, plates and glasses and cutlery clinking, phones glowing. Occasionally a face was still lifted up to the stage, briefly.

I was watching, alone.

She didn't perform. I could see that, in a very fundamental way, she did not particularly try. Somewhere at the centre of her she was calm and still, somewhat disappeared, absented. She became clear as glass. And the sound of the instrument did not originate from within; it came from behind her and moved through her. She was hardly even there. But it was extraordinary. Like a spare voice across a great distance.

I wondered about that. This warrior child with her tattoos and innocent face and complete lack of presence, which, turning itself around, became a presence of its own. No flash, no flourish. Unlike the sax player, who was really grinding, as they sometimes do.

The next song, "Bang Bang," kicked up and wove through the room. Nancy's version, just sax and keyboard. It was unsettling, darkly lonesome—whoever made the set list took their alcoholism very seriously—but the tables didn't notice. Truthfully, they rarely do. The night was still sparking.

I saw the man I had met Monday, and it took half a moment to remember his name. He was walking out from behind the bar, holding a bottle by its neck and the glasses tucked together in one hand, and taking a sudden swing to the left as he turned toward me. Al. He slipped between tables as if they didn't exist; when we made eye contact he smiled. I started to stand as he got closer.

"Peter, good to see you again," he said, setting the bottle and glasses on the tiny circle of a table and pulling his chair out. "It was a surprise."

"A surprise?" I started to sit back down.

He was sitting as well, reaching for the bottle. He peeled the top and pulled a small opener from an unseen pocket, vigorously plunging in the screw and twisting, vigorously popping it out, everything over in several smooth movements. "This is easier when standing," he said. I couldn't see how it possibly could have been easier—it seemed two or three seconds. He poured out two glasses, slowly. "Yes, surprising, because you didn't get the job."

"Lucia invited me."

"Yes, she says that to everyone. No one comes. But you did."

I reached for my glass.

"Lucia likes that," he added. "When people surprise her. When they show up." He lifted his glass to his mouth and then, raising his eyebrows at me, tipped it lightly toward me in a salute. "To showing up," he said, taking a drink.

I had a drink. "Thanks Al." It was nice, I looked down into the glass.

"It's a good one," he said.

"Well, send her my thanks too."

I looked back, behind Al, but didn't see Lucia anywhere by the bar.

The band shifted into some jauntier ones, Boris firing off the songs with the click-click-click of his sticks. Al and I didn't talk much; we sat close at the small table, drinking and watching the band. He filled our glasses again.

"You think she is good?" Al nodded up at the stage.

"Yeah, I do."

"She looks strange—the hair, the tattoos. But Lucia liked her."

I considered my words for a few moments. "She has a quality that's good for a trumpet player."

"What quality is that?"

The question was obvious but nevertheless I had not prepared for it, so I had to consider again. I had some complicated thoughts, couldn't untangle them, and the alcohol was slowing me. "She plays it very plain," I said. "But that makes it very pure."

Al tilted his head as he watched her play.

"It's a straight shot," I tried again. "If you know what I mean."

Al nodded. "I am not a musician like you or Lucia, but maybe I understand."

I could try to describe it to Al, but it wouldn't make sense; maybe someone like Billy, someone a little drunker and lonelier, would get it. A soft-hearted hippie would get it. I couldn't even quite explain it to myself. It was a loose collection of feelings and the thoughts and words were trying to follow, but I was always slow to the second half—the part of showing it to someone else. The assembling of words. And I was approaching drunk.

She had the bell tipped up, as if drinking from the air.

It was about performance, I guess—how common it was now. Not just here, with musicians, where it made sense, but everywhere; performance had shown up everywhere else in our lives and it just made everything lonelier. That was something I could never describe to Stasi about being online, how crowded and isolating it was, performing life instead of living it—the repetitive grief of ever actually knowing anyone in real life because they were never who they said they were. The smell of sweat. Everyone trying. Everyone watching, everyone wincing against strange, secret hurts. And the truth was I tried being online, but I just couldn't try like that, there was something dead in it. I couldn't just put short clips online, I had to present a whole Self—the performance was too much about the Self and the Self was so isolating. When artists got lost in it, they became bitter and small. I didn't tell Stasi that; I had just given up and told her I had never tried.

They were saying we were so lonely now, saturated with so many selves, writing articles about it, studying it, but nobody really changing anything, ever—just lamenting in a pathetic, non-committal way.

Pathetic, that painful word. Spending the day with Horse in my thoughts—the reliable stand-in for my grandfather, a shut-in and shattered man I barely knew. Those soldiers got PTSD from the slaughter of men in fields far from home; we were lonely and online. Pathetic was the second damage after the first damage was done, the humiliation of it. We never got called to anything great, or terrible; we were as separate as hard, round stones on a grey beach. And we bickered.

I saw something in the trumpet player, as Lucia had. She was different. She was a clear piece of glass, and whatever it was—the note, the song, how the room pulled in small around the sound—it shone straight through her with no clouding, no self, no colour in the glass. No performance. Humility and service to the music and nothing else. Servant, not master—and yet not shy.

I thought I was like that but I must have known somewhere I was not—dogged, my whole life, by the stain of self-consciousness. And the trumpet was too proud for that. The trumpet called for fearless servants. Immaculate pride—not in the self, but in the calling.

I wasn't good enough, I wasn't as good as her.

Al poured out the last glasses from the bottle, giving himself the shorter pour. "You want some bread?"

"No, I've had a lot already."

Al nodded as if it was a normal thing to say.

Around us, the room was mellowing, plates were getting cleared, people were sitting back in their chairs. Al was also leaning back, his hands crossed on his stomach as he watched the band. There was an easy quiet between us. Some of the early tables were leaving and new couples and groups were coming in; their bright eyes darted around the darkened corners of the room. There was the excitement of walking into a room where a band was already playing.

I didn't want to turn sad. It was too easy.

"So do you work here?" I asked Al. "Or just drink here?"

Al grinned at me, throwing his head to the side. He genuinely liked that. "I live here." He pleased himself with his answer too.

It was no use; I was going to turn sad.

Then, briefly, I wasn't. Then I knew, fatally, that I would.

But then it rose like smoke, and left—and then it came back, returning so honest and faithful. My heart was breaking all over.

I wanted to have a good night here but a shadow was collecting around the edges of my vision and I knew I would turn sad; it would start when Al left the table and move sharply downward with every drink. Or upward, depending on your alliances. A holiday song and some of the upbeat numbers had passed and the band shifted down into the Stones song; I had played it Monday, but now it felt years old. "I Got the Blues." Yeah. I was going to turn.

Al drained his glass and smiled at me. "It was good having a drink with you," he said. "You don't talk too much."

There was heat in my face from the red wine. "Thanks again." I gestured with my glass, still half full.

"You work in a kitchen?" He stood up and tucked his chair under the table, not looking at me until the chair was in place.

"Yeah, I do."

His face was serious now. It was hard to say which decade Al was in, fifties or sixties, but he was in the longish stretch in which the exact year didn't really matter. There was a hearty weariness in his face, alert and vigorous, but he was above it all. Bored but faithfully playful with life, an old cat batting something meaningless around. But now he was looking down at me, serious.

"We have a guy in our kitchen retiring next month. Been with us thirty-five years, earned himself a break." He smiled. "Anyway, you should call Lucia next week about it, because we will need someone new in the kitchen."

The song shuffled in and out of my hearing. Al tipped his head slightly in a neat bow and gestured with his hand—*goodnight*—then left with the empty bottle and his glass. He was gone, a receding figure disappearing between the tables. I followed him with my eyes and looked for Lucia around the bar; still, she was not there.

The trumpeter wasn't playing much in the Stones song either. She was mostly holding back. Sometimes she lifted the bell and let out a long note behind the sax, an aside, musing. Everyone was talking. Some faces stayed down for food and phones; servers slipped between the tables like slender, darting fish. The whole room was red. The whole stage was blue, a waterfall rushing down.

Al's words had shot a thin line through my veins, crackling through the heavy wine, confusing my thoughts at first, but they cleared quietly and left a space of great, expansive calm. I was a bit drunk, I was getting there, and not going broke for it either—next week was another world, and there was no comprehending it. It was cold outside, and that was a comfort to me in the great warmth of this room, the gathering pool in my body.

People were looking up. They stopped eating and looked up, some sitting back in their chairs. A server stopped for a half a moment, looking at the stage.

There was almost a pause in the room.

But it broke, and everything started up again—murmuring voices, glowing phones, the delicate din of glassware and cutlery bright around the room.

This trumpet player was good, though. She belonged to something outside her self. And the relief washed down like so much cool movement, eager for an end. I knew what I was seeing. Lucia had not picked someone unworthy—she saw it as I saw it, the final humility, service without performance. I had been so afraid I was wrong about it, and about Lucia. But I was right. White shirt luminous in the blue light, shoulders sloping down between notes, head sometimes hanging to the side. Listening. Relief, turning from cool to warm, suddenly rushed my eyes. The trumpeter was alone up there, and not lonely for it at all.

DECEMBER

IT WAS THE last smoke in the pack. For that reason, I knew it wasn't going to last. I had two phones in my bag, sleeping.

I never once mentioned the drunk, vague texts Mateo had sent, so it just died there, that open thing finally closing, scarring over. If he was hurt, I never knew, because he never showed. Probably not. His escape would surface again later in a different form, the same beast with a new head. At least I saw it coming and at least I had been practising what proved to be some version of peace for me—waiting.

Work was work. A third of my life, made of sand.

Christopher and Sarah remained the centre of everything and for that reason, an impenetrable and inanimate thing.

Four or five summers ago I was walking along a crowded street downtown, headed to a restaurant to meet friends, and I passed a car wreck; two cars ripped open on the street and everything stopped, everyone standing around them.

Red and blue lights strobed the street and the staring faces; the ambulances were loading bodies, mostly alive, but some were left in the street. If you pay attention you see how quickly it all ends—this life, this whole thing. And what did you do with it? There was a single call across this great empty lifetime and I heard only echoes of it, could never find the source.

So I smoked. I did not always like who I was but I was not going to hide. I was going to live—use up this life, spend it until broke—fully alive, bruised and aching, heart beating and breaking. Fully alive, alone.

* * *

She brought the bracelet back. It had been almost two months since the visitation.

Vanessa came to the door and had such kindness in her face that I blanked, in shock, before I understood she was holding her hand out to me. In her palm was a gold bracelet inlaid with white onyx and diamond—my wedding anniversary gift from years ago. "I think you left this," she said, trailing off. She gestured with her hand, asking me to take it.

"You knew it was mine?"

"Yes, you've been wearing it for years. It's noticeable." Vanessa looked at me carefully, her face at rest. She had those very large, quiet eyes that some people have, like deer. But she looked tired. In a way she looked gone.

She had put on a heavy coat to walk over but her head was bare and her wool-socked feet were inside bulky boots left unlaced. There was leftover snow from a storm a few nights ago. It was cold outside, and I felt the warm air rushing out the door behind me, and the cool air rushing in.

I couldn't help it. I felt the tears starting to slip down my cheeks, very slow.

I didn't cry, I didn't make any sound, and I could speak normally.

"I'm sorry about your girl," I said. "I didn't know what to do." Still the tears were slipping down.

Vanessa looked away from my face. "You didn't have to do anything," she said.

She looked down at my hand, still holding the bracelet, waiting for me to reach out. In that empty moment, I saw how much she had changed: eyes, hair, skin, everything. She didn't want the bracelet, but I didn't want the bracelet back—Vanessa saw it.

"Put it in a box and give it to Sarah when she's older," she said, gesturing again.

I took the bracelet from her hand and when we looked each other in the eye I saw a woman who had moved through immortal loss—she was a statue now. In her own way, gone. The grief had turned to stone and the rest of us moved through life like paper.

"Thank you," I said. "I will give it to her."

Without saying anything else she turned and went down the steps, then turned again and started walking along the sidewalk. Her unlaced boots were loud. But I knew she lived in the other direction—maybe going for a walk, I didn't know.

You didn't have to do anything. I knew, hearing it, that it would come back to me again. It seemed to say more than it said. *You didn't have to do anything.* I didn't have to try to save her from the grief; I didn't have to save anyone. *You didn't have to do anything.*

But I wanted to.

I took the bottom edge of my sweater and wiped my face.

ACKNOWLEDGEMENTS

For the book:

Akin: You restructured and renamed my debut—you're a genius, and a life-changing person.

Norm: I see everything you've done for me and then I multiply that across all your writers—another life-changing person. I hope we made a good book together.

Diane: You knew exactly what *The Clarion* was and you protected that. Then you made it better. Basically an ideal editor—every writer dreams of it.

Nate and Jason: Among my first readers, you made this book feel "real" after so much time alone with it. More importantly, your impressions and ideas were brilliant.

Aaron, Jason, Curtis: Unbelievable blurbs.

Megan, Jules, Mylène: I appreciate every effort, large and small, to publish this book.

Stu: You did the hardest work, and I'm grateful for your attention.

Gillian: I know I still took some creative liberties and I hope you forgive them—but thank you for your trumpet expertise and showing me what a real musician was.

Sarah: You don't know me, but I was working on my final draft with my editor while reading *Run Towards the Danger*, and I came across the Tenant League in PEI—the tin trumpets. It was a beautiful moment. So at the last minute, I put it in the book. Thank you... gifts from strangers are pure.

Douglas: Always my first reader, and my valiant defender, even against myself. This book does not exist without you. Nothing does, really.

For me:

Claire: The only worthwhile thing during my brief stint at university was meeting you. I've come to rely on you for everything—inspiration, advice, humour, name-dropping you and your adventures to people I've just met. It cost $20K to meet you but it was worth it.

Emma: So much childhood, so few friends. "Friends" isn't even our word... you were "my person" for the loneliest years of my life. I miss you.

My family and in-laws: Your enthusiasm and support for each minor milestone kept me going. I hope you are proud of me.

School Friends, Work Friends, Writer Friends, Everybody: Thank you for years and years of support, humour, and patience, and reading my longwinded emails.

Douglas: The first and last pages of my book carry your name. Thank you for our quiet life.

INVISIBLE PUBLISHING produces fine Canadian literature for those who enjoy such things. As an independent, not-for-profit publisher, we work to build communities that sustain and encourage engaging, literary, and current writing.

Invisible Publishing has been in operation for over a decade. We released our first fiction titles in the spring of 2007, and our catalogue has come to include works of graphic fiction and nonfiction, pop culture biographies, experimental poetry, and prose.

We are committed to publishing writers with diverse perspectives. In acknowledging historical and systemic barriers, and the limits of our existing catalogue, we emphatically encourage writers from LGBTQ2SIA+ communities, Indigenous writers, and writers of colour to submit their work.

Invisible Publishing is also home to the Bibliophonic series of music books and the Throwback series of CanLit reissues.

If you'd like to know more, please get
in touch: info@invisiblepublishing.com

Invisible